D0228367

Peter Taylor was born in Sedgefield, County Durham, and has worked as both a teacher and prison lecturer.

NO EASY TRUTH

For DI Don McIntyre, when it comes to Middlesbrough crime lord Tony Pike, it's personal. So when the murder of a local priest gives him the opportunity to nail his nemesis, he makes his plans accordingly. But even as he closes in on Pike, Don's personal life starts to unravel. What is his girlfriend hiding as she tries to distance herself from him? And what is the heart-rending secret that his father has been keeping for all these years? As Don struggles to uncover the facts, he is about to learn that there are no easy truths.

Books by Peter Taylor
Published by Ulverscroft:

VENGEANCE IN HIS GUNS
THE COURAGEOUS BREED
BLOOD QUEST
THE LONG RIDE BACK
THE BLOOD RUNS DEEP
STITCHED
DECEIVED
STONE COLD
A QUESTION OF LOYALTY

PETER TAYLOR

NO EASY TRUTH

Complete and Unabridged

ULVERSCROFT
Leicester

First published in Great Britain in 2016 by
Robert Hale Limited
London

First Large Print Edition
published 2017
by arrangement with
Robert Hale
an imprint of The Crowood Press
Wiltshire

A catalogue record for this book is available
from the British Library.

ISBN 978–1–4448–3159–7

Published by
F. A. Thorpe (Publishing)
Anstey, Leicestershire

Set by Words & Graphics Ltd.
Anstey, Leicestershire
Printed and bound in Great Britain by
T. J. International Ltd., Padstow, Cornwall

This book is printed on acid-free paper

Dedicated to my mother and father and also Vilma Hardy and Christine Smallbone, two ladies of substance who think of others.

Prologue

Ten-year-old Donald McIntyre squatted beside a pond in Middlesbrough's Albert Park watching the sun filtering through the trees to form a golden carpet on the water. Looking down into a mosaic of light and shade at the bottom of the pond, he saw a fish dart into sight then with a sinuous wriggle of its tail disappear again. In that moment, he was filled with a sense of contentment only a youngster can feel when he's been released for the school holidays, the prospect of many days of blissful freedom ahead. Life was good, he was happy and in his child's mind he thought it would always be like that.

'Come on, Don! There's a fight, man!' one of his pals called out as he ran past. His voice brought Don back into the human world.

Don hesitated a moment. Fights weren't a rarity in Grove Hill, Middlesbrough, where he lived. But other kids were running now and he was worried he might miss something, miss out when they were talking afterwards. With a last lingering glance into the depths of the pond, he sprang to his feet and chased after the other lads.

A crowd had gathered in the corner of the park. As he ran, he could feel the excitement in the air. It reminded him of his first soccer match at the Riverside Stadium with his father and brother Paul, that same sense of anticipation in the gathering crowd. Slipping through gaps, he made his way to the edge of the circle, saw two youths squaring up to each other. Struggling to believe the evidence of his own eyes, he realized one of the fighters was his brother, the other one Tony Pike, a feared ruffian. When they started on one another in a flurry of punches and kicks, Don stood there as though entranced.

Finally, he came to terms with the reality of what was happening. That wild look on Paul's face was something he couldn't associate with the brother he knew and, from the fury behind the blows being struck, he sensed this fight was on a different scale to others he'd seen. When Pike struck Paul's nose and it began to pour blood, a thrill seemed to pass through the watchers like an electric current. Don started to cry, cried even harder when his brother staggered under the force of a head butt. Wanting it to stop, he tried to step into the circle to pull Paul away, but strong hands thwarted his attempts, hauled to the back like a piece of flotsam caught on an incoming tide. Never before in his short life had he felt so helpless.

Occasionally, a gap would appear and he would catch a glimpse of the combatants' bloodied shirts and faces, but then the gap would close, leaving him ever more frustrated. The noise of the crowd escalated, as if those present had merged into one great roaring animal, an animal obeying an instinct he didn't understand and which was willing his brother to fight for its own gratification.

'Knife!' someone yelled and the animal fell silent. Then, when it started to roar again, it seemed to reach another level of voracious need.

'Stab him up, Pike!'

Don's heightened senses selected those words from all the other shouted comments. They sped down his nerve channels. He'd seen stabbings in films but that had been playing. This was different, he knew. This was real; his brother in dreadful danger. All the strength seemed to leave his body. He couldn't help himself. His legs gave way, knees buckling like a newborn colt's. Bawling his eyes out in fear and frustration, he lay on the grass, each roar of the crowd leading him to imagine the knife sinking into his brother's flesh. Why didn't somebody stop this? Why didn't someone save his brother?

'Bizzies!'

The word erupted from members of the crowd in a snarl. Then, as though a lash had been laid across its back, the animal gave a whimper and fell silent. Time seemed to stop as it disintegrated before Don's eyes, parts falling away in all directions as individuals ran from the scene. Finally, the amorphous beast was no more and only the two figures it had been feeding on remained, their eyes riveted on each other. Don saw something flash in the sunlight; realized Pike was holding a knife.

'Paul!'

Hearing his brother yell, Paul turned towards him. Pike, too, was distracted; looked away into the distance as though unsure what his next move should be. But the spell was broken. Lowering the knife, he smiled maliciously.

'You're lucky this time, McIntyre,' he said and ran off.

Don ran to his brother who, breathing heavily, put an arm around his shoulder. A drop of blood fell onto Don's face from Paul's nose; ran into his mouth so that he could taste it.

'Got to run, our kid,' Paul said, glancing at the policeman heading towards them.

They sped off together, made it to the thick bushes near the fence where they knew there was a hidden gap. As he squeezed through, Don didn't care much whether they were caught or not. All he knew was that his brother wasn't dead. In his heart, he blessed those policemen who had appeared just in time to save him.

They managed to make it home. Paul didn't go in with him; after making him promise not to tell their parents what he'd seen, he departed for a pal's house to get cleaned up. But if either of them thought that was the end of it, they were mistaken, because that night when his father arrived home from work he threw his bag down and ordered Paul into the living room.

From the kitchen, Don and his mother listened to the raised voices, his father's voice angrier than he'd ever heard it. His mother started lifting plates from the table in an absent-minded manner. Don knew she was upset and trying to hide it. Had his father found out about the fight? he wondered.

The voices eventually rose to a crescendo and the living-room door banged. His father's voice echoed in the hall.

'We'll be moving if you keep this up!'

His words proved to be true. Two weeks later, they were gone from Grove Hill and living in a large property in Wolviston, a village on the outskirts of Teesside. A few months later, the mother Don adored died of lung cancer. She was only thirty-seven years old. Another three bleak months passed and, persuaded by his father, his brother joined the army. For Don, life had changed dramatically. He and his father remained in the big house but he yearned for his old life and wished he could turn back the clock.

1

DI Don McIntyre never forgot that day in Albert Park, the tension in his stomach as he'd feared for his brother. Today, he could feel that familiar tight cord in his gut, pulling in opposite directions, as though a tug of war was going on down there. To add to his discomfort, the unmarked police car smelled bad. He knew why. Billy Liddle in the back seat reeked of whisky, aftershave and sweat, a triple assault on the detective's olfactory processes, faintly reminiscent of the clouds of ammonia that the wind had sometimes wafted across Middlesbrough when he was an infant. He guessed the whisky must be a necessary bolster to the snitch's confidence, an antidote to the fear he must be feeling.

'Van's late, Billy!' He could hear impatience in his voice. 'You're sure Pike will be driving, aren't you?'

Billy shuffled in his seat. 'Two of his geezers said so right in front of me, like I wasn't there, like I was the Invisible Man. Can't say fairer than that, boss, can I? I'm trusted, see. I done jobs for Pike.'

McIntyre sighed. He hated the gangster

Tony Pike with a vengeance, hoped he hadn't let his feelings override his judgement by trusting Billy on this. He'd been reliable other times, of course he had, but those other times hadn't involved Pike and Pike wasn't a man who took risks; he had risen above the level where he had to do the dirty work. Though he controlled most of the drug trade in Middlesbrough, he had his fingers in other pies too, but from a distance, too many layers to uncover before you could get near him. Was this business today going to be a slip-up that would bring him down?

'Pike's the driver,' Billy reiterated. 'He's dropping off the guys this time. They'll have gear on them to sell to their regulars.'

For the umpteenth time, the detective asked himself the question: Why would Pike choose to take a chance? Well, it was too late now to reconsider. What would be, would be. He'd pushed this operation because it was a rare chance and now everybody was primed and in place. It was all in the lap of the gods.

They were parked in a side street not far from the town centre, convenient, the detective supposed, as a dispersal point from which the street sellers could disappear to their different patches. Catching the boss and his minions in one haul was a dream. But the van was already late and his doubts reasserted themselves. Then, suddenly, just as he was almost ready to give it up as a bad job, the van appeared at the far end of the street, pulled into a parking spot not more than fifty yards away. McIntyre tried to stay cool and collected but his body wouldn't agree; he could feel his heart thudding against his ribs. He couldn't make out who was driving. He wanted to use his binoculars but he knew it was a risk and would give the game away if he was seen.

'Told you so, boss,' Billy chirped up.

McIntyre ignored him, picked up his radio and held it to his mouth. His eyes never left the white van. As soon as there was any action, he would set things in motion and the trap would close.

A minute passed before men started to emerge through the back doors — if Billy was right, ready to go about their dirty business on the streets. Daring to hope Pike really was involved, McIntyre yelled into his radio.

'Move in now!'

As though the street was a film set and he a director who had suddenly called for action, the scene came alive, his plain-clothes colleagues and uniforms scurrying into view from their hiding places. McIntyre watched them swarm around the drug dealers but a spark of satisfaction soon gave way to a feeling that something wasn't quite right. Why hadn't anyone tried to run? They'd all surrendered meekly and were standing on the pavement looking as innocent as a bunch of choirboys. Too easy, he thought. Far too easy.

His eyes shot to the van. One of his colleagues was yanking the driver's door open. This was the moment that counted. If Billy had it right, Tony Pike would step out any moment and be arrested. He'd go away for a long time, justice would be served and McIntyre could derive satisfaction from that, not least because at last he'd hit back at the gangster for the damage he'd done to his family all those years ago.

As he watched, the driver tumbled out of the van onto the pavement. Straight off, he knew it wasn't Pike. The man was far too thin, none of the customary arrogance in the body language. His spirit plummeted, the voice coming over the radio accelerating its descent.

'None of them are carrying. Doesn't look like there's any in the van either unless it's well hidden.'

McIntyre cursed. He'd set this up and now he'd have to carry the can. DCI Jimmy Snaith had reluctantly approved the operation. There was no love lost between him and his superior, who would have a field day with this. Worse than Snaith's wrath was the fact that Pike was still free, laughing at another failure to snare him. He already considered himself immune. After this debacle, he'd be even more sure of himself.

'Let them go,' he said forlornly into the mouthpiece. 'Call it off.'

Billy Liddle hadn't said a word. McIntyre's eyes lifted to the driver's mirror, fired daggers at the snitch as their eyes met. Billy squirmed in his seat.

'Cat got your tongue, Billy?' he snapped. 'Thought you were trusted, did you? Looks to me like you were set up, either that or you knew and danced me around.'

'Don't know what you mean,' Billy said, sounding affronted. 'I told you the truth, boss, on my mother's life.'

McIntyre sat on his temper. He couldn't be sure Billy had been two-timing him. It could well be someone else had informed Pike what was going down and, though he hated to admit it, it could well be a copper. After all, this wasn't the first time Pike had slipped the noose.

'I hope you aren't lying, Billy, because if I find out . . . '

As he spoke, he caught a movement in his wing mirror, someone approaching on the pavement. When he saw who it was, he froze in disbelief, then yelled at the snitch.

'Get down now! Flat as you can!'

Fast as a meerkat disappearing down its hole after spotting a snake, Billy squeezed himself between the seat and the floor.

The approaching figure drew level with the driver's door and halted. With a woeful sigh, the detective wound down the window and looked up into the face he detested. Eyes like small black stones set in a snowman's white face, and just as unemotional, stared down at him from either side of a nose that had been broken so many times it was now a passable imitation of a slalom run. The body was superficially fat but the detective knew that pudgy look was deceptive; beneath the fat, it was as battle hardened as the brain that controlled it.

'Mr McIntyre, as I live and breathe,' Tony Pike said. 'I hope you're not kerb crawling. Not with all your lads out in force. Could ruin your career.'

McIntyre, forcing himself to remain cool, grunted. 'Your career will go down the pan before mine, pal.'

Pike's grin showed a set of perfect white teeth that would have looked fine on a male model but in his face was as incongruous as icicles in a desert.

'The good guy will triumph over the bad

guy, huh? That old baloney. Look around you, Donald, and I think you'll agree the evidence of such outcomes is sparse. Bit like believing in the tooth fairy, if you ask me.'

'Move on, Pike,' McIntyre replied, waving a hand dismissively. 'Today you'll survive . . . but there'll be a time. Meanwhile, suck in that beautiful Boro air while you still can.'

Pike shook his head, feigning disappointment. 'Why do you keep antagonizing me?' he said. 'Going after my guys like you have. You know if I'm not in control of business there'll be chaos — crimes will soar. It's fear of me that keeps the petty little punks in line. Remove me and you'll get gang warfare. You've seen it happen in the movies, yeah?'

McIntyre stared at him with contempt and said nothing. 'What? You still can't have that against me! We were young. Not my fault if your family chose to leave. Time you forgot all that.' Pike winked knowingly. 'I could do you some good, you know.'

The detective snorted. 'I never forget a thing, Pike, especially all those lives you've ruined.' He sighed. Why was he bothering? All this banter was simply degrading. 'Get out of my sight,' he said. 'There'll be no compromise with the likes of you.'

Pike took a step back. His lips formed a make-believe pout. 'Suit yourself. One day you might be happy to change your mind.'

'That a threat?'

Pike narrowed his eyes to slits, tilted his chin. 'You . . . and yours . . . know better. I don't threaten . . . I act!'

The detective tightened his grip on the steering wheel. His knuckles showed white, an old memory of Pike flailing at his brother that day in the park resurfacing.

'That's how a man is known, by his actions. Yours speak volumes about the devils inside you. Myself, I can't decide whether all those beatings you took from your father twisted you, or you're a freak of genetics.'

Pike's fists clenched but he kept them by his side. For a moment, the detective thought he wasn't going to keep them there, that he was going to open the door and haul him out, administer one of those beatings that had made him a feared man. But instead he took a step back, the knowledge he was dealing with a police officer no doubt acting as a restraint and cooling his ardour.

'There's two kinds of people,' the gangster snapped, 'the strong and the weak. In this world being strong is all that counts. You're weak like your old man. That's why he took your family away and that's why you're grubbing in the dirt, satisfied with a copper's pay.'

14

By luck or design, Pike had hit a nerve. The barb about his old man went in deep. McIntyre camouflaged it with a blank expression, then forced a slow smile.

'Pike, you're big, hard, possessed of more animal cunning than a hunted fox with the pack at its heels . . . but you're forgetting your limitations.' The detective tapped his head with his finger. 'In there, that's where the real strength exists and ultimately why you'll fall. There's so many good guys brighter than you, see, and you're too thick to know that.'

Pike didn't reply, just stood there, clearly fuming. Then he started to walk away and McIntyre thought they were finished until he halted after a few steps and faced him again.

'Talking about brains!' Pike tapped his head in an imitation of the detective's gesture. 'Wasn't so bright of you to let your old man move back to Grove Hill. Both of you must think it's not dangerous for him there any more, like it's a health spa for the elderly or something.'

Before the detective could reply, Pike smirked, spun on his heel and strutted away, shoulders rolling, head in the air, the self-styled king of the Boro walking proud in his kingdom. Exasperated, McIntyre watched him go. There'd been no gain from all that verbal sparring, only a meagre, childish satisfaction derived from baiting the gangster. All said and done, Pike was still the man and today had been a disaster.

That last remark Pike had thrown at him had hit home. Why indeed had his old man chosen to come back to the place he'd grown up? Was he trying to prove something? If he was, it was too late for that now; all he was doing was giving his son a big headache. Pike's last remark had illustrated that.

He'd been so engrossed with Pike, he'd forgotten Billy until the snitch stirred in the back and hauled himself onto the seat. Turning to face him, McIntyre saw fear in his eyes, beads of perspiration on his brow. He looked frightened enough for the detective to believe he definitely hadn't known it would all go wrong this morning.

'Good job those windows are tinted, Billy, eh!'

Billy blew out his cheeks. 'You kept him talking long enough. I was sweating buckets back here.'

'Don't worry, he showed no sign he knew you were there. You should thank your lucky stars for that.'

'He was waiting for you,' Billy said, a tremor in his voice. 'He knew!'

The detective raked a hand through his

hair. 'Yeah. He knew.'

'One of yours!' Billy sneered. 'A bloody, bent bastard copper.'

Billy's alliterative summary was crude but McIntyre empathized with the sentiment and the tone of voice. Bad enough he'd had to endure the gangster lording it over him without the possibility it was one of his own who'd sold him down the river.

He thought the snitch's indignation was too sincere for him to be involved, but he wasn't so naïve as to dismiss the possibility entirely.

'I heard what I heard,' Billy continued, in a mumble. 'Must have changed plans last minute.'

'You so sure they didn't set you up?'

Billy looked affronted. 'Naw, man. Always ahead of the game is Billy Liddle. Careful, like.'

McIntyre thought the snitch was overestimating his abilities. Small-time criminals usually thought they were cleverer than they were, their self-regard leading them to underestimate other people's intelligence and acumen. It usually led to their downfall. In this case, it could mean Billy ending up on the bottom of the River Tees.

'Drop me somewhere else, boss,' Billy said. 'Just in case any of Pike's lot are hanging around.'

The DI started the engine and set off down the street. The van was being searched as they passed it and a cluster of uniforms were standing on the pavement. Embarrassed, McIntyre raised a hand and waved tentatively but their response was lukewarm. This morning had been a waste of time and had given Pike's lackeys a chance to laugh at them, boast how they'd made fools of the boys in blue, and they didn't like it.

He dropped Billy in the car park on top of the Cleveland shopping centre, in a bay that was permanently in shadow, like the snitch's life. Billy assured him he would be all right.

'Go canny for a while and watch your back,' he said as Billy made to get out.

The snitch looked him in the eye. 'And you watch all your mates, boss.' He scowled, added without any sense of self-irony, 'Hate grasses, me, especially if they're bizzies. Backstabbing bastards are just hypo . . . critters. Least I am what I am — a professional.'

On another occasion the detective might have found that little speech amusing but not this time. He watched Billy slink off, his body language so different to Pike's; no ostentatious roll, more like a shy creature of the night, shoulders caved, head moving side to side, alert to his surroundings as though there were dangers lurking others couldn't see. The

DI wondered how his nerves stood it, guessed that was the price he had to pay for his double life; more fool him because the retainer the police paid him, the reason he must think himself a professional, was no way commensurate with the danger. But he couldn't feel too sorry for him; it was his choice, he knew the score, was a petty criminal who'd hurt people in his time. Today his insouciance had been mostly bravado; deep down he must be worried about the turn of events.

Back in the traffic, he went over the failed operation, looked for flaws but found he kept returning to the conversation he'd had with Pike. It was a consolation that he was causing the gangster headaches, satisfying that Pike knew why he was being so assiduous in pursuing him. With that thought, his mind returned to the day his brother Paul had fought Pike and its aftermath. He'd heard much later that Pike's father had given his son a hammering in front of his mates for not being able to beat Paul before the coppers arrived to end the fight.

Unfortunately, no matter how much he tried to dismiss it, his perception of his own father had changed that day. As well, he'd woken to the fact that there was no supernatural power on the side of the good;

innocent people suffered, it was a fact of life. The people who succeeded against evil, to an extent, were the police. That day in the park when they'd come to the rescue probably influenced his future choice of career. If there was a God, he figured, He needed men to protect the innocent. McIntyre always kept that in mind when the job frustrated him.

2

Bill Clancy edged the door open, put his head through the gap, stared at the little boy who stood on the doorstep, just for a second believed that his eyes weren't deceiving him and it was Tommy standing there. The moment of self-delusion soon passed.

'Can I see Tommy, please?' the boy said, looking slightly perplexed since all he could see was the man's head.

Clancy's eyes bulged in their sockets as though any moment they would explode. His glower clearly frightened the boy, who took a step back.

'Who put you up to this?'

The boy's bottom lip trembled; tears rimmed his eyes.

'I'm D-David . . . ' he stammered and, half turning, raised a small arm to point behind him. 'I live over there. I've been away all summer and . . . '

'Get away with you!' Clancy barked. 'Tommy's gone. He won't be coming back . . . ever!'

The boy needed no second bidding. He pirouetted and sped down the garden path as though he'd just encountered a malicious

21

ghost and was afraid it was following only a whisker behind.

Clancy slammed the door, walked back down the hall. It came to him suddenly that David had indeed been one of his son's friends and he felt ashamed, had to fight back tears. The boy, only an infant, couldn't have known what had happened, hadn't deserved to be on the receiving end of his vitriol.

He entered the kitchen, slumped down in a chair. Hunching over the electric fire, he stared at its two red bars as though mesmerized. In his heart, he knew very soon he'd have to move out of this house. The memories here were haunting him every day, mocking him, like welcoming arms reaching for him, only to be withdrawn when he thought he was entering their embrace. He was afraid, if he stayed, the depression he was battling would one day swarm over his defences. There would be no telling what he would do then. His treatment of that boy had surely been a symptom of his state of mind. All that was keeping him going was force of will, the same will that had served him in that other desolate place where, day after day, he'd stared at other bars, then, as now, seeing nothing ahead for him other than an aching loneliness. Restless, he wandered to the window, looked out into the garden, noticed the washing line swinging in the wind. For a moment, he thought he saw her standing there, stretching to hang out clothes, at her feet their lovely boy, the centre of their lives. She'd called him a miracle from God sent to bless them. How wrong could you be?

It was too much to bear. He turned away, slumped in the chair, rubbed his eyes in an attempt to remove the bittersweet vision from his brain. But his dear ones wouldn't leave, came to him hand in hand, the boy looking up into his mother's face, so trusting as they ascended the narrow metal steps. He watched in dread as they reached the top of the bridge and looked down at the River Tees, the wind ruffling their clothes and hair like a mischievous sprite urging them on. Then, the unthinkable, both of them plummeting, breaking the surface of the dark water to vanish into nothingness. A shiver as cold as those waters ran up and down his spine like the devil's clutch. Would that soul destroying vision always haunt him? Would he always wish he could follow them down to those depths, never return to this vacuum which felt like a prison, this time without bars?

'Where are you now, Priest?' he cried out. 'Where are you now when I need you most . . . more than I ever did before. Why haven't I seen you?' He thumped his fist on the table in frustration. 'Is it because you know there are no words that will help me so you've washed your hands of me?'

The question tormenting him as much as those terrible visions leapt into his mind. Did the priest consider he was responsible for his wife and son's tragic actions? Since it was an accusation he'd laid against himself often these past weeks, could he blame the priest if he did? He'd lost his job, been miserable about that, doubting he would get another one; felt emasculated because he wasn't providing for his family the way he wanted to. Mary and he had argued about it occasionally, but there was nothing he could think of that could have led her to that bridge, to that terrible decision.

Perhaps he'd been deluding himself that they'd been a happy family. Mary had talked about going back to college, felt sure her sister would help look after Tommy if she did go back. Had her fortitude, her optimism about the future been forced? Did she regret she'd ever met him? It had seemed nothing short of a miracle to him that a good, beautiful woman like her, who deserved and could have had the best, had settled for him. Darker thoughts visited him. Was God punishing him for his past, for daring to imagine that with a woman like Mary at his side he could expunge that past, better himself in this world? Was that why Tommy had been taken away from him so cruelly?

When he thought of his wife pulling Tommy down into those watery depths, he hated her as much as he loved her, a dichotomy that tore at his nerves, threatened his sanity. Exhausted, he was aware he couldn't ride this emotional rollercoaster much longer. In the end, if he didn't do away with himself, he had only two choices: endure no matter how bad the pain or go mad. For certain, life could never be the same again; the happiness that had taken years to find hadn't lasted and he doubted he could ever find it again . . . or even wanted to. If he was to go on, he'd have to excise those happy years as best he could. Maybe the best way to do that would be to go back, imagine he'd just been released, do what he would have done if he had never met the priest, or Mary. For a start, he could find the man who'd been responsible for putting him in prison and robbing him of those two years, knowing he was innocent. After he'd taken his revenge, he'd let life take him where it would, as though he'd never been on a better road.

Making up his mind, he rose grim-faced out of his chair, picked up a black plastic bag and went through to the front room.

Tommy's toys were scattered just as the boy left them. He hadn't been able to bring himself to touch them yet. Though he knew the idea was nonsensical, he'd allowed himself to hope that as long as they were there his son might come back. Gritting his teeth, he steeled himself, picked them up and dropped them in the bag. Next, he swiped the framed photographs from the mantelpiece, and with a groan thrust them into the bag too. That wasn't the end of it. His brain in a no-man's-land where no sentiment was allowed, he moved like an automaton from room to room, filling three bags with things that might remind him of his loss.

When his miserable task was complete, he carried the bags into the garden and piled them up. It was beginning to get dark now; silhouettes of the trees swaying in the breeze as though they were mourners watching in sad complicity as he lowered his head and said a half-hearted prayer of farewell, out of respect for his wife more than any conviction he would be heard. Finally, he fashioned a makeshift torch from newspapers, lit it, threw it onto the pile. Not able to watch the flames feasting, he trudged back to the house with pieces of windblown ash swirling around him like fragments of a torn love letter that would never be pieced together again.

3

After the morning's debacle, McIntyre kept his head down and stayed in his office typing up his report, seeing his failure laid out in black and white, reinforcing his irritation with himself. Most of the remarks his colleagues had fired at him on his return had been jocular but in the end wearisome. One piece of luck, though, was that DCI Snaith was away on a management course. Boy, did he need it, thought McIntyre. Apparently he wouldn't be back until late afternoon at best — or at worst, depending on your point of view. With that knowledge in mind, McIntyre slipped out of the office early, though he knew he was only postponing the inevitable rollicking, which would be hard for him to take from a man he didn't respect.

His flat was in Marton on the outskirts of the town, the birthplace of Captain Cook, the explorer. When he arrived home, he changed into his running gear and went for a two-mile jog around nearby Stewart Park. Surrounded by expanses of green grass and trees, for a little while he managed to forget his bad day. Afterwards, he showered and lay down, hoping to catch up on some much-needed sleep. That night he would be meeting friends of Kate, his girlfriend, and he wanted to be at his best.

As he was drifting off to sleep, Kate was on his mind. She was in charge of an old folks' home, Done Roaming, in Grove Hill and he had come to admire the way she handled the clients, never patronizing them, always polite, but firm with them when she had to be. From his point of view, the relationship had been progressing well these last two months and he hoped it was the same for her, though he did have the feeling — although had no solid evidence to back it — that she didn't particularly care for his profession. Or was he just being paranoid and what sometimes he took for her antipathy was merely indifference?

Feeling better for sleep, he rose two hours later and, casually attired in open-neck shirt and sweater, set off as the evening was drawing in. Kate lived in a flat attached to the home, about ten minutes away. Marton Road, a nightmare at rush hour, was quieter now and he soon reached St Peter's, the church Kate and the residents attended most Sundays. There, he turned off and headed into Grove Hill. As always when he drove this way, he recalled happy days of his boyhood.

When his mind cast up less pleasant memories, he shut them out, considering he didn't need to give himself any more grief today.

Something flashing bright in the driver's mirror gave him a start. Then another flash came and he saw a fork of lightning streak across the sky behind the church spire, a scene straight out of an old horror film, usually heralding doom. The rain announced its arrival with a drumbeat on the car roof and he was grateful he'd been sufficiently pessimistic to put an umbrella in the car.

The rain became a relentless onslaught. Suddenly a woman ran across the road in front of him, dressed only in a flimsy blouse and short skirt. Hindered by her high heels, she stuttered along the pavement, the rain hurling silvery spears at her as though it bore her a personal grudge. McIntyre drew level and saw her face; thought he recognized it. Those features were more worn and a little harder than he remembered but he was sure he could see the young girl she'd once been beneath make-up and mascara running down her cheeks. He was nearly past when one of her heels caught and she measured her length, banging her head on the wet pavement as she sprawled like a footballer tackled unfairly from behind. He pulled over, got out, gripped her arm and helped her up. In spite of protesting she could manage without help, she was clearly shaken, so he ushered her into the passenger seat.

'Take a minute,' he said, climbing back into the car.

She took deep breaths and dragged back her hair. Then, as she wiped her face with the handkerchief he handed her, she looked at him properly for the first time. He thought he saw a spark of recognition in her eyes.

'Don't worry, love,' she said. 'I've been hit harder and survived. That was a midgie bite.'

She gave him a weak smile, which revealed a missing tooth. He pointed to it.

'That was a punch, love, not the fall,' she commented. 'The punch was worse than any fall.'

She made to get out but he could see she was groggy and could be concussed, though a sudden whiff of whisky made him unsure of the real cause of her clumsiness. Whatever, he couldn't send her back out into the pouring rain in that state.

'I'll take you to A and E,' he said. 'You look well out of sorts and it's always best to be sure when you've had a bang on the head.'

She turned her face towards him, gave him a quizzical stare. 'A and E can't fix what's wrong in this head.' She placed the point of

30

her finger on her temple. 'I'm a walking, talking accident and emergency, me. Best you drop me at my friend's house. It's just up the road.'

'If you're sure,' McIntyre said, doubtfully. In truth, he was a little relieved. He didn't want to be late when he was meeting Kate's friends for the first time.

She gave him directions and it was only a couple of minutes before he pulled up in front of a terraced house she said was her pal's. He opened his door, intending to get out and help her, but she tugged at his sleeve.

'Don't think you should,' she said. 'Won't do my street cred any good being seen in the company of a policeman with your reputation, Detective Inspector McIntyre.'

He gave a wry little grin. She knew him, then, just as he had known for sure who she was as soon as she was in the car.

He pointed to his temple, imitating her earlier action. 'Nothing wrong with your brainbox after all, eh! Didn't think you'd remember me, Joan Burton, not when you were the goddess of the school and I was just a wee boy.'

Her eyes lit up with amusement. 'Goddess! Been a big fall from grace for me, then.' She reappraised him. 'They say you're a hard copper who doesn't give an inch but you've been kind to me and with nothing to gain.'

He laughed. 'Except I got to sit next to a goddess for a few minutes.'

'Didn't think anyone would recognize me from those days,' she said, smiling.

'You were a few years older than me, a very pretty girl in my brother's year.'

'Paul McIntyre was your brother, wasn't he?' He nodded sadly and she said, 'I know . . . he was a good sort and the good die young.'

There was a brief silence. A faraway look came into her eyes. He thought he must have sparked off memories, a wistfulness for those bygone days, for that long-gone schoolgirl. But she soon snapped out of it.

'You know what's happened to me since then, don't you? Why haven't you mentioned my descent to the dark side? No copper's that sensitive, surely.'

He broke eye contact, stared at the windscreen. Raindrops were meandering their way down the glass, leaving a complicated web behind them.

'Pike,' he said, turning back to her, his face blank.

She smiled and the gap in her teeth was like a cave in a jagged white cliff.

'Got it in one, Detective. Pike happened to me!'

'You're still with him. Never broke away.'

It was a statement, not a question, and she raised her eyebrows. 'My my! I won't need a biographer when I'm famous, not with you around.'

He hadn't intended to go down that road, yet something compelled him to persist. 'What hold has he got on you, Joan?'

She reached out and with the tip of her finger traced the path of a raindrop as it ran down the windscreen, then suddenly hovered as though not sure of its direction.

'He doesn't give a monkey's about me, hasn't for a long time and the feeling's mutual.' She gave a resigned sigh. 'He keeps me around for the same reason he always did — a bit of decoration. I stay because he feeds the craving he gave me when I was a girl and it doesn't cost me.'

'Drugs.'

'You know that,' she snapped. 'Don't pretend you don't.'

The rain pattered on the roof. McIntyre thought it a wonder, with her history of drug abuse, that she still retained much of her looks. But for how much longer? He could sense her melancholy, surmised their conversation had reminded her of happier days, better roads she might have chosen. He watched her tilt her chin, pull her shoulders back, defying her brief moment of self-pity.

'You could have left Middlesbrough,' he said, 'and you still could. I can arrange for detox, no strings. There's a place . . .'

She turned towards him. 'Grove Hill is my home. I won't leave it. No way.' Her tone turned sarcastic. 'You can afford to be patronizing. Your family had the money to run away from Pike, tails on the ground. Don't think I don't remember that, Inspector.'

Her words stung. His auntie had always insisted his father had done right moving the family. The trouble was McIntyre had loved his life in Grove Hill, in spite of the place's rough reputation. It hadn't been easy losing his boyhood pals and adjusting to the village environment. All that upheaval because of Pike! Worse, it hadn't finished there because his father had persuaded his beloved brother to join the army, fearing Pike would get to him one day. Joan Burton must have seen the hurt in his eyes because she was quick to apologize.

'Sorry. That was unfair. You're only trying to help me, I know.'

'Forget it,' he grunted. 'It was all a long time ago.'

'Another lifetime for you and me.'

He nodded. She was right; it was another

lifetime. But people remember; Joan wasn't unique in that. Why did he still feel a sense of shame?

'The offer still stands,' he said. 'Accident and Emergency, I mean. It's up to you. Can only advise, not force you.'

She dropped her eyes to the footwell and rubbed her head. When she turned her gaze back to him, she didn't look sure. Her indecision showed in her frown, the down-turn of her mouth, the faint tremble in her hand. He thought she might capitulate but instead she pulled herself upright and, looking straight ahead, felt for the door handle.

'Thanks, but no thanks. I'd better be off now before you try to get me to join the police force.'

'Well, if you're sure,' he said, as she opened the door. 'But take care.'

She gave him an appraising glance. 'You too. You're nothing like they say you are, by the way.' She added mischievously, 'Nearly as good-looking as your Paul but not quite.'

McIntyre swallowed. The way she'd mentioned Paul's name in that light-hearted manner, it was almost as though he was still alive.

'It was hard when Paul was killed in Iraq . . . sniper fire . . . nineteen years old.'

35

After he'd said it, he wondered why, figured it was because it was rare these days to meet anyone who remembered Paul from the old days. She seemed to understand his feelings.

'I'm so sorry,' she said, touching his arm. 'I didn't mean to remind . . . He was a nice lad.'

She said no more, just climbed out of the car, thanking him for his trouble. He watched her all the way to her friend's door, the rain battering her, her head bowed against it. He felt sorry for Joan Burton, but the feeling was tempered by the knowledge that it was her choice to live in a criminal's world and she could break away if she chose. His brother would have been exactly her age now if he'd lived. That thought brought a feeling of regret and not a little anger. Pike and his father: in different ways they had taken his brother away from him.

4

The gathering was in Roberto's Pizza House in Linthorpe Road, not far from the town centre. McIntyre and Kate had joined the party of ten, which consisted mainly of people she knew from the various agencies connected with her work. Kate was sitting opposite him. Pictures of tranquil Italian lakes hung on the restaurant walls. The romantic, seductive tones of an Italian tenor came from speakers. If he half closed his eyes and tried to shut out the voices around him, he could almost imagine he was alone with Kate on a balmy night in Italy — instead of the Boro in the rain.

The truth was he didn't care much for large gatherings, his preference the company of three or four folk he knew well. Tonight, however, he told himself he should make a bit of an effort, step out of his comfort zone, create a decent impression for Kate's sake. Kate was driving so he could have a good drink, hopefully relax into the company.

The woman sitting next to him, plumpish, probably in her mid thirties, seemed pleasant enough and diverted the conversation into general topics in an obvious effort to make him welcome. One or two of the others were not so convivial; talked shop, leaving him out of the loop. His mind drifted until Kate drew him back, addressing her remarks directly to him. He hoped his moments of inattention hadn't been too obvious.

Suddenly, the guy sitting next to Kate, who had been staring at McIntyre in a way he considered not dissimilar to people he'd arrested who thought they could get one over him, addressed him in a snide tone.

'So, Inspector Montalbano,' he said, raising his eyebrows, 'what's it like being an officer of the law in the wild northeast? Not so hot, I should imagine!'

The tone attracted attention. Conversation died away as eyes turned to McIntyre, waiting for his reaction. The guy himself was grinning. His patronizing bestowal of the name of the fictional Sicilian detective was obviously a source of self-amusement. McIntyre might have just been able to take it, except he sensed a challenge here, which rankled. For some reason, the fellow wanted to put him down in the company. His eyes flickered to Kate and he lowered his eyebrows.

'Gilbert, as usual you're being rude,' she responded, tight lipped. She smiled at

McIntyre. 'Don't take a bit of notice. He's like that with everybody.'

McIntyre slid his eyes back to the man and nodded. 'Got it, Kate. Just his way, huh?'

Two waitresses arriving at the table to pour wine provided a diversion and the awkward moment passed. McIntyre downed his second glass, then settled into his margherita, only managing a few bites before Gilbert struck again.

'Must be hard to switch off when you're a bobby,' he stated, addressing the remark to Kate but his voice loud enough for all the others to hear. 'Must always be watching people, waiting for them to slip up.' He grinned slyly in McIntyre's direction. 'Bet your friend is sussing us out right now.'

Kate coloured up, ignored the remark, warned Gilbert with an angry frown, then poured the woman next to her a glass of wine to hide her irritation. McIntyre bristled but decided, for Kate's sake, to guard his tongue. He sensed the guy wouldn't leave it there, was on a roll. That instinct proved to be true because a moment later he spoke up again, addressing him directly this time.

'That Inspector Montalbano,' he opined. 'His creator made him a bit of an amateur gourmet who refused to talk while he was eating — that was the only time he really switched off apparently.'

With slow deliberation, McIntyre wiped his mouth with his napkin. For sure, this wasn't his day; it had started badly and it wasn't done with him yet.

'I'm half Scottish,' he said. 'In the Highlands it's customary to carry a wee hip flask of the hard stuff when you go to dances and such.' He paused, the eyes of the company riveted on him. 'Your earlier remark was correct, Gilbert. I am always watching . . . so I couldn't miss the hip flask you removed from your pocket earlier as you went to the washroom.' He raised a quizzical eyebrow. 'Strictly medicinal, I presume?'

His target coloured up, gripped the edge of the table, digging his fingers into the wood as though clinging to a cliff edge. But he wasn't deflated enough not to persist.

'Bravo!' he muttered. 'You've proved my point.' He raised his hands, made the shape of a camera with his fingers. 'Click! Click! Big Brother is always watching us, even when we attend to our ablutions.'

There were a few half-hearted titters. Kate's look implored McIntyre to leave it there but he wasn't finished.

'Medicinal intake aside, you've had two and a half glasses of wine, old boy. Plus, as we came in, my eagle eye happened to notice the tax disc on your vehicle is two weeks out of date.' He picked up his knife and fork, cut his pizza with surgical precision, let his eyes drift around the room. 'But I'm a nice guy really and this is a pleasant little gathering, so enjoy.' He fixed Gilbert with a hard stare. 'Only be sure to make your next drink a soft one, in case one of my even bigger brothers is watching and pulls you.'

The meal resumed and the verbal jousting didn't seem to have soured the atmosphere. McIntyre made a greater effort than usual to be amenable, hoping to redeem himself, recover any ground he might have lost with Kate. He even spoke pleasantly to Gilbert, who, surprisingly, seemed to recuperate pretty quickly. Kate didn't show any sign that she was harbouring any ill feeling and he could only hope nothing was simmering under her placid exterior. The others in the group didn't shun him; they paid him more attention if anything.

After the meal, they were sipping coffee when one of the women in the group described how an acquaintance had been burgled recently, her living room trashed by the intruders who were drug addicts. Gilbert caught McIntyre's eye and spoke up, his tone matter-of-fact rather than challenging.

'Even if they catch them, they'll just put

them in the clink, utterly fail to rehabilitate them. Am I right, Donald?'

Not seeing any traps in the question, McIntyre responded. 'If an addict commits a serious enough crime, he should go to prison. Most crimes are committed by a small number of recidivists who don't respond to help anyway.'

He sensed the plump woman next to him stiffen. When she spoke her voice and manner were censorious.

'Surely you're not saying we should give up on those who succumb to drugs, those poor souls who have been beaten down by life and . . . lost themselves.'

Heads nodded in agreement, including Kate's. Too late, he remembered these people weren't his own colleagues who might have endorsed his view; foolishly, he'd broken his rule to never, on occasions like this, get involved with matters which touched on his work. He noticed Gilbert's eyes glinting at a fresh opportunity to reassert himself, which he just couldn't ignore.

'Prison clearly doesn't do enough to deal with causes of criminal activity and can't deal with the underlying causes of addiction,' he pontificated. 'It's a primitive system and surely that's why there are repeat offenders.' His eyes darted to McIntyre. 'What do you think . . . really?'

McIntyre was stubborn. Though he read Gilbert's intentions, why should he avoid contention, surrender meekly to this creep? Even slightly inebriated, he felt he could hold his own.

'Prison fails to deal with causes of criminality because it's not meant to be primarily therapeutic or medicinal but punitive,' he stated.

Gilbert leaned forward, a half smile playing on his lips as he swivelled his head to look along the table, making sure he was the centre of attention.

'So you agree with that, do you, Donald? In all conscience, you can lock addicts up, then forget about what happens to them next.'

McIntyre hesitated. Gilbert was trying to show him up and there was no way out. Nothing for it then but to put the idiot back in his box.

'You obviously aren't aware a vast number of addicts are criminals before they're addicted and that no totally reliable cure exists.'

There was a brief silence until Kate, who he noticed had kept a poker face as the sparring resumed, surprised him.

'I think addicts do commit crimes because they are addicts and wouldn't if they were their true selves!' she snapped.

Feeding on her words, Gilbert smiled triumphantly and turned the screw.

'Donald, it sounds to me like you've fallen for establishment propaganda.'

McIntyre shook his head. He didn't like the way Kate had spoken to him, the way she was looking at him, the way the others were staring at him as though he was a pariah. But he wasn't prepared to give it up.

'Contrary to popular belief, in prison many addicts break their habit. Unfortunately, as soon as they get out they revert.'

The creep reacted with a slow, satisfied smile. Kate was white, staring at him with what he thought was something approaching disdain. Surely she wasn't as angry with him as she looked. When she spoke, her eyes bored into him as though daring him to defy her.

'You don't mention going to prison can leave a scar for life on those who can't cope . . . on gentler souls. It's too cruel for them.'

'Hear hear!' someone else intoned to murmurs of agreement. 'It shows a society lacking compassion and generosity of mind.'

McIntyre realized now he was wasting his time. Clever Gilbert had known his audience, even Kate, too well.

'It's easy to be lenient at other people's expense and call it generosity of mind,' he

44

responded. 'Forget there's always a victim to consider.'

Gilbert smirked. He'd lit a fire; now it needed stoking.

'It's mostly the rich who are robbed,' he said, 'and that's a reflection of the indecent inequalities in our society, the 'have nots' trying to restore the balance.'

' 'Fraid not,' McIntyre rejoined, deciding it was in for a penny, in for a pound now. 'Most addicts rob people who can ill afford it. The rich can replace losses. Anyway, what's happened to compassion for the victim . . . any victim?'

Nobody took him up on that, not even gleeful Gil. What kind of game had he been playing? Was he simply one of those people who liked to agitate for the sake of it? To McIntyre's relief, the topic dried up and the conversation swung away to other matters, though he participated only in a perfunctory manner, feeling the company had judged and condemned him. Kate didn't speak to him again and he was sure he'd unwittingly offended her. When the evening finally ended, it was a relief. He'd messed up and was angry for allowing himself to be enticed so easily onto hostile ground.

Driving back, Kate was quiet, too quiet, and aborted his attempts to engage her in conversation with monosyllabic answers. It was obvious something was brewing so he shut up, hoping it might pass. When they arrived at her flat, bad vibes emanated in his direction like invisible waves. Normally, he would go in with her for a coffee, sometimes spend the night. Tonight, as soon as they reached the door, she spun on him, her eyes glinting in the moonlight, no hint of softness in them.

'Was that really you tonight?' she snapped.

He spread his arms wide, opened his mouth, clamped it shut again and tried to think of a suitable answer.

'Really me? What do you mean?' he muttered eventually.

'No compassion! Hard!'

That angered him, confirmed what he'd thought was going on in her head.

'It was the plain truth I spoke, nothing to do with compassion. Surely — '

'I think we should have a break,' she interjected, without giving him a chance to finish. 'We're different people. I was worried about going out with a policeman in the first place.'

McIntyre's hackles rose. 'Oh, come on, you're being unfair. If anyone deserves your anger, it's that guy. I was a guest and he was out to pick a fight. I might have laid it on a bit thick, allowed him to goad me.'

She averted her gaze. By the light of the moon he could see her face clearly and suddenly he knew why Gilbert had been obnoxious towards him.

'Don't tell me! He's an old boyfriend, isn't he?'

She tilted her chin defiantly. 'I went out with him a few times . . . as a friend. Nothing in it.'

His mouth twisted into a sardonic grin. 'But he hoped there would be. Now I understand what was bugging him. He knew what buttons to push.' He let out a sigh. 'Looks like he succeeded in his purpose — setting you against me.'

'It was you and your attitude to drug addicts,' she said, 'not him. The way you spoke anyone would think you were God Almighty. Addicts have souls, you know, and they can get better.'

'I never said they couldn't. I had to — '

'It's late,' she interrupted, fumbling in her bag and handing him a key. 'I think you should use the guest room or walk home because I don't want to be near you any more tonight.'

He sensed it would do no good arguing, that nothing he could say would shift her. Maybe whatever was bugging her would seem different in the cold light of day. Reluctantly, more than a little bemused, he shook his head to convey how wrong he thought she was, then turned on his heel and with a curt goodnight stormed off in the direction of the annex and the guest room.

He retired to bed in a miserable mood, tossed and turned, worried that, without him even knowing, he had become as unfeeling as some of those he had to deal with. But deep down he knew that wasn't true. It was mainly the victims for whom he felt compassion. They would always be a priority in his mind. As for Kate, his instincts told him there had to be more to her sudden hostility than was apparent and, until he knew what that was, there would be a barrier between them he'd have difficulty breeching.

5

Father Brendan Riley fell clumsily into a chair vacated earlier by one of his students and tried to steady his breathing while he tried to come to terms with the big shock he'd had. Then, like a man possessed, face contorted in disgust, he tried to rub away the grey powder that covered his skin and clothes. Finally, realizing it would be too difficult to remove it all, he slumped back in the chair, the shock of how close he had just come to death hitting him like a hurricane.

He could still see the look of hatred as his attacker pointed the knife at him, hear the hissed threat to cut him into little pieces. All his excuses seemed feeble, built of sand, as he felt the heat of that fury coming at him like the fires of hell. The words had penetrated body and soul, like a voodoo curse that would never leave him. Even as his breathing returned to normal and he stopped shaking, it was those words that stayed with him, lacerating his soul. Would it not have been better if the knife had ended his life there and then, spared him the agony of conscience?

When he tried to rise, his body protested.

He felt completely defeated. Why had God made him this way? Why couldn't he escape his nature? He'd confessed, done penance, but to what purpose? He'd have to move on, start again. In that dark moment when all seemed lost, an epiphany came to calm him. Why had God stilled the avenger's hand, let him live? he asked himself. Surely it was a sign telling him he had to move to a place where he could be truly cleansed of his sins. Those vituperative words were his punishment and would go with him, his cross, his penance on those dark nights when he lay alone and heard Satan's overtures carried on the wind. Through grace, that torment would be his catharsis, resistance his way back to the path of salvation. Yes, a fresh start was what he needed. Everything happened for a reason. He was surely meant to move on.

He lowered his head to pray for himself and his tormentor, to give thanks for another chance. Footsteps echoing in the corridor interrupted his efforts. His pulse quickened. His body grew rigid. Paralyzed by the fear that his tormentor had returned, he kept his head down even as he heard the footsteps enter the room and continue towards him. Only when they halted directly in front of him did he drag his eyes upwards.

The face he saw was as rigid as a mask. All

the requisite features of a face were there but he could see no humanity in it. The eyes were focused on him but as though they weren't really seeing him because the mind was preoccupied with another purpose. The priest only had a moment to notice these things, but it was long enough for him to realize his fate was sealed and there was to be no reprieve after all. The arm holding the blade moved like a piston, thrust the steel into his stomach.

The knife withdrew. Pain came at him in waves as he looked down. Like blessed wine he'd sometimes spilled on pristine commun- ion cloth, blood stained his white shirt. He sought those cold eyes in a last, desperate plea for mercy but knew it was useless. A strange acceptance, a feeling of relief almost, came over him. He realized his burden had been too great, his flesh too weak to carry it. Maybe, at last, he would be able to find the peace that had eluded him on this earth.

'You won't escape . . . your . . . conscience,' he groaned. 'Believe me . . . you won't . . . I know . . . '

The killer thrust again, withdrew the knife a second time. Darkness came surging towards the priest now, devouring the light. His last thought, as the world receded, was that he hoped God would be merciful.

6

The morning after his argument with Kate, McIntyre drove back to his flat early, his mood not much better than when he'd left her the previous evening. When he'd knocked on her door she hadn't answered, though he was pretty sure she was inside. In the end, he'd given up, pushed the guest room key through the letterbox and driven home. He showered, shaved, grabbed a piece of toast and a cup of coffee then drove into town, still confused over Kate's attitude.

He sat in the headquarters car park for ten minutes trying to clear his head. Inside the building, Snaith would be lurking, ready to pounce on him, and he needed to be sharp witted because it was a pure fact he and the DCI didn't get along. He was never comfortable with the man. Years ago, as a sergeant to Snaith's DI, he'd been involved in a house raid and come across his superior in a bedroom, tucking something that could have been a packet of drugs into a drawer. They'd stared at each other for a moment, then gone about their business. Nothing was ever said but if ever he'd seen a guilty look it was the one on Snaith's face that day. He suspected Snaith had been planting drugs to gain convictions, make him look good. Mainly because he cultivated senior officers at every turn, Snaith was promoted quickly. With no love lost between them, McIntyre was sure the DCI would be pleased if he messed up big time.

He eventually entered the building and made his way to his office. Harry Thompson, a young, fresh-faced DC, said good morning and stood in front of him, barring his way. He was fidgeting as though he had a confession to make but was afraid to begin. McIntyre scowled and finally Thompson enlightened him. 'None of my business, sir, but I just thought you'd like to know the DCI is in your office.' Looking embarrassed, Thompson hesitated; it was clear he wanted to say more but was unsure.

McIntyre knew the DC wasn't the obsequious type, building up points with his boss. He thanked him, then said, 'But what aren't you telling me, Harry? Out with it, man.'

'Think he's in a bad mood, sir. Went at a couple of guys with both feet off the ground, studs showing, soon as he walked in, then he demanded to know where you were. Think he's in a real grump, sir.'

McIntyre was quite flattered by the young man's concern. Like everybody else, he would know about yesterday's fiasco, the likely cause of Snaith's irritation. Whatever, he wasn't going to show the DC he was overly concerned, nor comment about a senior officer to a junior rank, because that kind of thing did nothing for morale and undermined discipline in the long run. Instead, he tried to make light of it.

'Don't you worry, Harry, I put three pairs of shinpads down my socks before I set off this morning. That should do it.'

'Sorry, sir,' Thompson mumbled, obviously not sure he'd done the right thing. 'Thought it best to tell you he was waiting.'

McIntyre smiled, started to walk away, then remembered something and halted. 'By the way, Harry,' he said, voice lowered conspiratorially, 'you know that new girl in the office, the one the boys are all going wild about?'

The DC coloured a little. 'Y-yes, sir.'

'Well, I heard a whisper she fancies you but you didn't hear it from me.'

The young DC turned a deeper shade of red than a Boro football shirt; didn't know where to look.

McIntyre smiled and winked at him. 'One favour deserves another, eh! Forewarned is forearmed. Go canny with that one, DC Thompson.'

McIntyre's smile faded as soon as he turned his back on his colleague. He'd made an effort to make Thompson think he was unperturbed but as he headed for his office, his mood soon metamorphosed into something much darker. Who did Snaith think he was? He might be his superior but he had no right to enter his office when he wasn't present. Basic manners should have dictated that.

The DI's anger wasn't helped when he entered and found Snaith standing beside a cabinet leafing his way through a file which he'd extracted from one of the drawers. As soon as he saw McIntyre, he hurriedly returned the file and closed the drawer. In a scene reminiscent of two gunfighters facing each other down in a western, McIntyre eyeballed him until he looked away. Had the DCI deliberately arrived early so he could have a snoop, find something he could use against him? he wondered. Or was he just being paranoid?

'Morning, sir,' he said, just enough over-emphasis on the word 'sir' to make it sarcastic. 'I trust you found my filing system up to scratch.'

Snaith ignored the comment and gestured

towards the chair behind the desk.

'Be seated, Don!' The tone was that of a man who believed his rank gave him divine rights over his underlings. 'I suspect you know the reason for my visitation this morning.'

McIntyre eased himself into his chair and met Snaith's glower with an outward show of indifference. With his silver hair, fresh face, pristine white shirt and creaseless uniform, the DCI looked every inch the perfect embodiment of how a man of his rank should look, a man to inspire confidence if you allowed first impressions too much credence. McIntyre couldn't recall much Shakespeare but a line from *King Lear* had always stayed with him: 'Robes and furred gowns hide all.' Snaith's immaculate exterior definitely couldn't mask the fact he was a poor leader of men and all the management courses he'd attended had failed to remedy that weakness. Still, no matter how he felt about the man, McIntyre figured he'd have to nibble a morsel of humble pie after yesterday's non-event.

'Don't worry, I know it was disastrous and I regret it.'

Snaith tilted his head back, looked down his nose and snorted his indignation.

'Is that all you have to say, Inspector? As I recall, you assured me your intelligence was to be trusted. Now it turns out otherwise, wasting time and manpower that could have been usefully employed elsewhere — not to mention the expense!' His silver eyebrows descended in a frown. He thumped the desk theatrically. 'It's just not good enough. You've made me look . . . incompetent.'

McIntyre listened, trying to keep his temper. Did the DCI want him to get down on his hands and knees, kiss his feet, beg forgiveness? Well, it wasn't going to happen. Instead, he shrugged his shoulders.

'Some you win, some you lose. There's always that risk, sir.'

His phlegmatic attitude served to further agitate Snaith. An incandescent red tide ascended his cheeks, travelled all the way to his forehead, flowed into his silver hairline where it vanished like fire unable to traverse a snowy waste.

'Watch your attitude,' he snapped. 'It's near insubordinate.'

McIntyre let out a tired sigh. 'Look! Pike knew! He was even on the spot to gloat at my expense. That was hardly my fault, was it?'

'I suppose you can back up that assertion with facts, DI McIntyre, or are you just making excuses for your own shoddy preparation?'

McIntyre shook his head in frustration.

'You and I both know the snitch was always reliable. Why would a van appear with all Pike's minions inside, just as he said it would, then it turns out they were just out for a drive, all pals together? To top that, Pike appears from nowhere, walks right up to my car.' McIntyre stared hard at his superior. 'He knew, I tell you. The only question is how?'

'According to your report, Liddle was in the car with you. Is that right?'

McIntyre sighed. 'Yes, and he was genuinely scared. I don't believe he gave us duff information at Pike's instigation or he wouldn't have been so shaken up.'

Snaith rolled his eyes. 'But you can't be sure of that, can you? Even if Liddle was straight with us, which I doubt, if Pike saw him in your car you've jeopardized a valuable commodity.'

McIntyre fought down his anger. Obviously the DCI had made up his mind he was to be the scapegoat and would write his report with that bias. Nothing he said would make a difference.

'When I get Pike and his cronies, the truth will out,' he muttered.

'When I get, Pike, eh!' Snaith repeated scornfully. 'And just when will that be, pray? I'm beginning to think, Inspector, that the only pike you'll ever catch is one that lives at the bottom of a pond, has big eyes and scales on its back.'

McIntyre bridled at the insult. 'Maybe we should take that allusion further and say it's unnatural the way he slips off the line whenever we get near him, how he knows where not to swim.'

Snaith's cynical expression indicated as well as any words that he thought he was being naïve.

'I'm afraid your failures are making you paranoid, DI McIntyre. Pike is taking up far too much of your time, making you obsessive, in fact. I want you to focus more on your other workload from now on, in particular a case that's come up which I think will fully engage you, divert your mind into a healthier place.'

It was the last thing McIntyre wanted to hear. Pike's intrusion into his early life had led him to hate those who thought they could ride roughshod over other people for their own gain. He'd joined the force in the belief he could make a difference. Yet he had to admit it was the bare truth that, where Pike was concerned, it was personal as well. Maybe at times that clouded his judgement, as Snaith implied. The pity of it all was he was beginning to get under Pike's skin, chip away at his enterprises, let the gangster know he couldn't afford to be complacent or he'd sink. Now Snaith had put his oar in and there was nothing he could do about it except listen as he outlined his new task for him.

'Last night,' Snaith began, 'I set up a team to investigate a murder at Teesside University. A Catholic priest, Father Brendan Riley, was stabbed to death. He was teaching history part-time, had just finished his evening class when someone walked in and did the dirty deed. There were no witnesses. I've set up an Incident Room, allocated personnel. SOCO are already beavering away. Interviews are well on. Just read the policy book and bring yourself up to speed. You're taking over from here on in.'

In spite of his disappointment, McIntyre's interest was piqued. This was an unusual case given the location and the victim's profession. But his initial interest was tempered because he knew Snaith. There had to be an ulterior motive, other than the one he'd been told, for giving him the case. Could it be he was being handed a poisoned chalice?

'Have the press been informed?'

'Not yet . . . but they'll be on it soon enough. Make no mistake, Inspector, I want your full attention on this. The murder of a priest will gather a lot of interest in the media, so no slip-ups.'

The ensuing silence seemed to amplify the antipathy between the two men. Neither had any more to say. The DCI stood up and walked to the door where he paused, one hand grasping the handle. His lips manufactured a smile but his eyes didn't even begin to comply. When he spoke his tone was softer, more conciliatory, which only served to make McIntyre suspicious.

'Don . . . I know you and I are . . . '

'Different, sir . . . as in chalk and cheese,' McIntyre said, finishing his sentence for him, his voice as sharp as a rapier thrust.

Snaith breathed in deeply. 'Precisely, but don't think I would allow that to affect my judgement, prejudice me against you. We need all kinds in the force — variety enriches us.'

In his mind, McIntyre was reaching for a sick bag. The man was a chameleon. When it suited him, he could drip so much grease into a conversation it seemed to exude from his every pore. He was merely saying what he thought he should, in spite of their enmity. Probably he was remembering something he'd learned on that management course the other day, practising it like it was a game. Why on earth was he bothering when the line between them was drawn so clearly?

'You mean life is like a box of chocolates, sir.'

Snaith lost the smile, replacing it with a quizzical look.

'Tom Hanks made that rather saccharine observation in the film *Forrest Gump*, sir. Thought perhaps that was where you got the concept . . . you know, variety enriches. Right now I'm thinking brazil nuts, truffles, chocolate fudge, orange creams.'

Snaith shook his head. 'You are a wag, aren't you? Good job I have a sense of humour, though I wouldn't advise you to push it too far.'

With that, Snaith exited and McIntyre breathed a sigh of relief. It was some consolation that he hadn't been removed from Pike's case entirely, though no doubt this new murder investigation would consume his time and he wouldn't be able to hassle the gangster's operations to the same degree. For sure, most of his colleagues would have leapt at the chance to lead the inquiry into the priest's murder. What was Snaith playing at? He wasn't in the habit of doing him any favours. In fact, he was sure the DCI would rejoice if he asked for a transfer; he would much prefer new blood he could bully and mould in his own image.

7

McIntyre spent the next two hours in the Incident Room familiarizing himself with the priest's murder, reading through the policy and action books, listening to taped interviews and introducing himself to relevant personnel. Then, anxious to view the scene himself and touch base with the team, he set off for the university campus.

Situated close to the town centre, it wasn't far to drive. As he drove onto the campus, he noticed young people carrying files or bags, a purposefulness about them which was good to see when too often he dealt with youths who lived aimless lives. Of course, there were those who rose above the mire, resisted the peer pressure or the lure of drugs to follow their aspirations, but for every one of them he met in the course of his work there was another who spiralled downward.

After he parked up, it didn't take long to find the scene of crime. Police tape festooned the entrance to the building and a couple of uniforms stood on duty outside, a picture that seemed incongruous in this world of academe. But he knew well enough violent acts were not the preserve of low-lives, intelligence no guarantee people could control their baser emotions.

One of the uniforms directed him towards a building where the team were gathered. As he made his way there, he was aware of students standing in groups to stare and speculate about the police presence. Seeing the young faces, McIntyre felt his age, as though he belonged to another world far removed from theirs. He could sense an enviable camaraderie amongst them and thought it a pity it wouldn't survive when they entered the world beyond the campus and other responsibilities took their toll.

The room his colleagues had commandeered was just a large classroom with a whiteboard covered with diagrams and names. Uniforms and plain clothes were working at desks. He didn't interrupt as he passed through them, just nodded at those he recognized.

DS Moira Hogan, one of the inquiry team, rose to greet him. She was thirty years old but looked so youthful she could have passed for one of the students. Under that exterior, however, McIntyre knew she was a no-nonsense Irish woman who somehow juggled two kids and a husband with the job. Reliable and loyal, she was good at it too. He enjoyed the banter with her because he knew she would never take advantage.

Moira tilted her head at him, wrinkled her freckled nose. 'So you're DCI Snaith's blue-eyed boy these days, sir.'

McIntyre scowled. 'From that remark, I gather you all know already I'm in charge. Well, Moira, you can rest assured my eyes aren't blue and I must have been the last one upon whom the DCI wanted to bestow his boundless munificence.'

'Would you like me to brief you now, blessed one?'

'I'd like you to show me the crime scene first, Moira.'

'You don't want to form too many preconceptions before you've examined it?'

'Exactly. Did that with too many beautiful women in my time. Should have taken a closer look first instead of letting their appearance deceive me.' Grinning, he added, 'Present company excepted, of course. You always lived up to my first expectations, Moira.'

Moira pulled a face. 'Didn't realize you'd kissed the Blarney Stone.'

Minutes later, dressed in protective clothing, they passed under the police tape, made their way past the lift, negotiated four flights of stairs, turned into a corridor and entered the second room on the right. The scenes of crime boys were still hard at work. One of them, Jim Brady, whom McIntyre knew, sauntered over.

'Corpse has gone to the mortuary,' he said, pointing to the shape of a body chalked on the floor. 'The pathologist said two stab wounds.' He indicated an area of his stomach. 'Here, very close to each other. He'll be doing the autopsy today but, given the body temperature, he estimated the victim died around nine last night, death almost instant.'

Though he'd already read up most of that info and would need to contact the pathologist anyway, McIntyre thanked him and pointed to a bloodstained chair just outside the chalk outline. All the other chairs were neatly tucked under desks.

'I gather he was sitting in that chair when he was stabbed and fell. Is there anything else you can tell me, Jim?'

Brady pointed to two men working on their knees a few yards away. 'We've bloodstains, fingerprints and footprints. That's a last sweep they're making now. Everything we've got is on its way to the labs.' He angled his head to the side. 'And now your next question is the one I'll still be hearing in my next life should my creator choose to punish me.'

McIntyre didn't disappoint. 'How long for results? Forget about the next life. Sometime in this lifetime would be good.'

The SOCO laughed good-naturedly, then sighed. 'Couple of days, best guess. But don't get your hopes up. This room is in daily use, lots of bright young things passing through, so we might not get anything distinctive, except, if we're lucky, a drop of the assailant's blood . . . or a fingerprint . . . maybe.'

McIntyre pulled a face. 'Any good news?'

The SOCO's eyes sparkled like two diamonds. 'One thing! Saved it till last deliberately to cheer you up.'

'The anticipation is killing me.'

'Well, you'll like this. It's a new one on me. The corpse, and a bit of floor too, were covered in a grey powder which the pathologist thought was made up of crushed bones, would you believe. He'll obviously confirm, or tell you otherwise, when you call on him.'

McIntyre and Moira exchanged glances. This was different; might turn out to be one for the annals. A priest stabbed and covered in powder sounded like a ritualistic killing. Perhaps the murderer had a religious, or anti-religious, mania and hated priests. The powder was interesting but, of course, finding the murder weapon had to be a priority and teams were out searching the campus as they spoke.

Moira said, 'There were personal effects found — a jacket hanging on a peg next to the whiteboard, a wallet containing money in one pocket and a mobile phone in the other. The jacket and wallet are at the lab, the mobile with the tech boys. We'll probably be able to learn who the dead man's contacts were. That might be helpful.'

'I take it there are CCTV tapes, Moira.'

'Yes. DS Macdonald has made a start there, sir.'

'Good, we'll leave that with him, then.'

The DI turned to Brady. 'Thanks, Jim. I'm sure talking to those of us at the sharp end has lifted your morale.'

Brady made a face. 'Suffice to say you inspire a tad more enthusiasm than Snaith does.'

McIntyre grinned. 'That's what I call being damned by faint praise, Jim lad.'

8

McIntyre's next port of call was the morgue where he hoped big Bob Bell had completed an autopsy. When the detective rolled in, he found the pathologist at his desk, biting a chunk out of a sausage sandwich, tomato sauce spilling out of the sides like blood oozing from a wound.

He didn't learn much more from Bob than he had from Jim Brady. The deceased was around the thirty mark, had indeed been stabbed twice in the stomach and died within two minutes. The mysterious powder covering the corpse was in fact ash, weirdly the remains of a body that had been cremated. McIntyre's initial thought was that it would yield DNA, but was disappointed when Bell informed him that bones were ground to ash after a cremation and it was impossible to extract DNA from ash. He was glad the business with the pathologist was short, if not so sweet. Something about morgues didn't agree with his stomach and the smell of that sausage combined with the dollops of tomato sauce skirting the edges of Bob's mouth hadn't helped.

Back at headquarters, he was in the Incident Room musing on potential news headlines the press would think up, things like, 'Police investigation reduced to ashes', when Moira filed in with four detective sergeants he'd called for a briefing. The strain of working into the early hours showed in their grey faces and he felt a little guilty, as well as at a slight disadvantage, coming to the case after things were already well in motion.

'Appreciate you're hard at it,' he began. 'But I want to make sure we're all on the same page, so bear with me while I run through what we know.' He cleared his throat and continued. 'First, the victim is a priest, Father Brendan Riley of St Peter's Church, Grove Hill. A caretaker found him dead at the crime scene at 9.15 p.m. Two cleaners on the bottom floor were the only other people in the building at the time. A Mr John Bright, a lecturer at the university who'd been teaching in the adjoining lecture room, left at 9 p.m. and was the last person to see the priest alive. Both his class and the victim's class had left at 8.30 p.m. CCTV shows a woman in a hood entered the building carrying a black bin liner at 8.50 p.m., ten minutes before John Bright left. She departed four minutes later at 8.54. Those are the basics.'

DS Spark, rotund in appearance and

blessed with a name that didn't reflect his laidback manner, spoke up.

'Have you listened to the interview tapes, sir? We did the caretaker and the cleaners on the spot; the lecturer at home.'

DS Macdonald, a hatchet-faced Scot, chirped up. 'That Bright geezer struck me as a cold fish and full of his own importance.'

McIntyre had formed the same opinion, listening to the recording.

'Thought so myself, Mac,' he said and added, 'I presume the students who attended the classes were all interviewed.'

DS Bird, known to the criminal clientele as 'the beak', for obvious reasons and not because of any irony in his perfectly proportioned nose, answered. 'Done and dusted. Both classes consisted of four Open University students, mature men and women. All eight left together and stayed in the Victoria pub until 10 p.m. Nobody left the company in that time.'

'So that eliminates them,' McIntyre said. 'The caretaker swears the cleaners never left the bottom floor, so that leaves our lecturer, the woman on the CCTV and the caretaker himself as our main focus for now.'

'John Bright reckons the priest was alive at 9 p.m.,' Spark stated, 'which would leave a gap of fifteen minutes until his body was discovered by the caretaker. If we presume neither man is the killer, someone went up without the domestics noticing, stabbed him and escaped unseen. If Bright is correct about the time, it couldn't have been the woman on the CCTV because she left before 9 p.m.'

'And the CCTV doesn't show anybody else entering or leaving the building in that time frame,' Bird said, tiredness making him sound irritable.

Macdonald chipped in. 'The cleaners, both women, were on the bottom floor working together and say the caretaker was chatting with them until he went up and found the body. The question is, did he find a corpse or create one?'

McIntyre had allowed free flow but now he interceded. 'Let's look into backgrounds and keep open minds for now. Mac, I know you're working through all the CCTV tapes. Any further comments?'

The Scotsman cleared his throat. 'The woman seems as camera shy as Greta Garbo, that old actress that hid from the world. She keeps her head down, moves faster than whisky down my gullet.'

'Keep going through all the tapes, Mac, see if she appears outside the building, or in another one. Look out for anyone else acting suspiciously.'

He turned to the others. 'Make sure anyone who was on campus last night is questioned. Moira will help there and she'll arrange for posters to go out in the area. Meanwhile, in case you think I've put my feet up, I'll do follow-up interviews, starting with the caretaker and the lecturer.'

'Do you want me to arrange for them to come here, boss?' Moira asked.

'Please, Moira. That would be best. Thanks, all of you, for your patience. I know you're tired. I also know you're professional enough, so I won't insult you with a speech about how important this is. They're all important and you know it.'

Birdy pointed a finger upwards. 'Don't worry, we'll be getting help on this one, the victim being a priest.'

Macdonald feigned disgust. 'That's pure blasphemy, man.' He lifted his eyes to the heavens. 'Please Lord, don't let him watch any more episodes of yon *Psychic Detective*.'

Birdy wasn't slow to come back at him. 'This from a man so archaic he remembers Greeting Garbo, whoever she was.'

The others laughed and there was more banter, which was good for the morale of tired men, so McIntyre let it continue for a while before he wound it up.

'DCI Snaith recently informed me we need

variety in the force, gentlemen,' he announced. 'I don't think he meant psychic detectives but if you have any strange visitations in connection with the case, DS Bird, I'm sure he'll be only too pleased to listen to you.'

They all laughed and Mac said, 'Don't you worry, Birdy, Greta will come back to haunt you.'

9

In the late afternoon, McIntyre stood by the window of his office waiting for Edward Wilson, the caretaker, to arrive. Sometimes, away from familiar surroundings, and especially in a police station, people reacted differently and he hoped he might be able to elicit something from him he'd neglected to mention the previous night.

His immediate view encompassed a cluster of businesses and factories that had sprung into life near the banks of the River Tees, known as the Middlehaven regeneration site. A little further away, huge towers and chimneys sent smoke signals curling lazily into the sky to be conscripted into the mosaic of dark clouds. This view he saw every day and there was nothing attractive about it, especially on a dull day when the sky was an unremitting grey and the river like a sinister black snake, slithering its way to the North Sea. It was a stark contrast to the west coast of Scotland where he spent his holidays and he often pictured in his mind the rugged green hills and the sea lochs further north. On occasions, mainly when work seemed like a huge beast devouring every hour of his day, he wondered about moving up to the Highlands. A little job chasing sheep rustlers, or seeking out illegal whisky stills while breathing in that fresh air, would be right up his street.

But he knew he was being fanciful; didn't think he would ever move away. Middlesbrough and its environs had too many memories of his brother. Even after the passage of time, he could still feel his presence, hear his voice. It was though part of Paul was still in this place and, if he left, he would lose him entirely. Of course, his father was here too. It was all far too sentimental, he supposed, but potent enough to have a hold on him.

A knock on the door interrupted his reverie. A portly, middle-aged man with grey slicked-back hair and a woeful expression followed a young policewoman into the office.

'You must be Edward Wilson,' McIntyre said, shaking the man's hand then gesturing to a chair opposite his. 'Please take a seat.'

'I'm the caretaker,' Wilson said gruffly as he slumped into the chair like a reluctant schoolboy beginning his least favourite lesson.

'I know who you are,' McIntyre said. 'I'm

Detective Inspector McIntyre. I've asked you here as an informal follow-up to last night's interview. Some of my questions will be repeats so please bear with that.'

The caretaker shrugged, his face impassive. 'Well, I'm on work time now, getting paid anyway, so fire away.'

Sensing small talk would be wasted, McIntyre began by keeping his initial questions perfunctory, mainly confirming what Edward Wilson had told his colleagues already. The man was adamant that the two cleaners had never been out of his sight before the classes left and he ascended the stairs and discovered the priest's body. Then, suddenly, just as the detective was going to move on to more delicate ground, the man surprised him by initiating a change himself.

'I suppose you'll have me in the frame for this,' he grunted, his lower lip protruding. 'Much good it'll do you.'

McIntyre stared into his eyes. 'That's very frank, Mr Wilson. You are in the frame but no more than anyone else we're interviewing.'

Wilson shuffled in the chair. 'Well, I'm not guilty, so not bothered what you think or do.'

McIntyre wondered why the man was being so defensive, brusque and dismissive. Was he was frightened and trying to hide something? In his experience, that was often the case with people who overreacted. Perhaps he was just one of those grumps you sometimes encountered who, in their arrogance, considered pleasantness to others an unnecessary social skill, superfluous to his way of life. A bit more probing was needed to gain a better measure of the man before he would know what was bugging him, so he ignored the attitude and carried on.

'Did you know Father Brendan Riley?'

'I knew who he was, yes, and what he was and what he wasn't.' Wilson grinned wickedly but why he'd done so was for himself alone to know, not for sharing with the detective.

'Didn't move in his circles,' he continued, with a sniff. 'Priests and caretakers don't mix socially. I clean floors, see. He was supposed to cleanse . . . souls.'

McIntyre found the man's manner and tone disconcerting, considering they were discussing a dead man who'd been brutally murdered.

'You never met him except in the course of your work? Is that what you're saying?'

Wilson broke eye contact, seemed perturbed. When he answered, his voice was almost a snarl.

'If you're any kind of a detective, you must have gathered I don't like priests!'

McIntyre leaned back. The man's candour

78

had taken him by surprise. Why was he being so forthright?

'Perhaps I did gather that . . . but that wasn't what I asked you, Mr Wilson, was it?'

His eyes locked on to McIntyre's, who decided to keep quiet and wait him out.

'I was Catholic, born and bred,' he said eventually, spitting his words out. 'Then those priests did what they did to my lovely daughter and I lost my faith.'

The strength of his emotions was almost tangible. McIntyre continued to probe, keeping his voice gentle.

'What exactly did they do to your daughter, Mr Wilson?'

The caretaker stared down at the floor with such intensity it was as though he was seeing all the way down to hell itself. When he did speak, the gruffness was gone, the voice more forlorn than angry.

'My Linda was seventeen . . . a child. She was pregnant and she was going to marry her boyfriend. The local priest wouldn't take the service. She tried two more and neither would they. Her boyfriend was a Muslim, you see. He made the mistake of saying, while he would convert to Christianity, his child would not be baptized, would choose its own religion. Those priests questioned the sincerity of his conversion.' Wilson winced at the memory. 'It was a conspiracy. I'm sure it was.'

A silence followed, grew until it felt like another presence in the room, heavy and brooding. McIntyre pressed him again.

'Is there more, Mr Wilson?'

The caretaker looked at the detective, his eyes full of spite, as though a demon had possessed him.

'Linda killed herself out of shame. She was religious, you see. Instead of showing compassion, those priests made her situation worse. She was too sensitive, my Linda. She had a nervous breakdown, took an overdose.'

Now McIntyre understood the reason for his unpleasant demeanour, felt sorry for him. But he put his emotions aside and tried to maintain a professional attitude because a motive was emerging and he needed to follow it through.

'But Father Riley wasn't involved, was he?'

Wilson recoiled as though he'd been physically struck. His lower lip curled.

'Riley was the third priest . . . the third betrayal,' he grunted, glaring at the detective as though daring him to deny it.

The caretaker was full of rancour and unlikely to stop there, McIntyre thought. He waited and sure enough he wasn't able to hold back.

'Who do they think they are? They're just

flesh and blood like the rest of us . . . ashes to ashes . . . dust to dust in the end. They sin like all of us. My Linda made one mistake and she . . . '

Overcome, the caretaker couldn't finish his sentence, lowered his head and started to weep. He'd revealed a wound so painful it would probably never heal, but was that pain strong enough to lead him to murder a priest who he considered wronged his daughter? Surely it must have been hell for him to work in such close proximity to the man. Had an opportunity to kill him presented itself and, unable to control his festering fury any longer, he'd seized it? His use of the biblical 'ashes to ashes, dust to dust' resonated eerily with the discovery of the powder in the murder room and on the body.

The caretaker rubbed his eyes and stared vacantly straight ahead as though there was a sheet of frosted glass obscuring his view of the world.

'You never get over a thing like that,' he mumbled. 'The waste.'

'Did you notice anything unusual about the priest's body or around about it?' McIntyre asked softly.

Wilson squeezed his eyes shut, opened them again, shook his head. 'All I remember is blood pouring out of his wounds and that he looked grey . . . grey as a gravestone. I've seen dead bodies but never that grey before.'

McIntyre wondered if he knew the grey was down to the ashes thrown over the priest.

'One last question, Mr Wilson, and then we're done for now. Did you notice anyone else in the building, anyone you didn't know . . . after the classes left?'

The caretaker shook his head. 'Never saw anyone.'

McIntyre nodded. 'Well, then, that'll do. Thanks for your help. I apologize for reviving sad memories.'

The caretaker rose, made for the door with his head down like a man following a coffin. He halted there and turned to address the detective.

'I know what you're thinking.' That gruffness had returned to his voice. 'But you're wrong. I'm an angry man inside . . . but no killer.'

With that parting shot, he exited and McIntyre sat there thinking he'd heard so many criminals deny their guilt, even when the evidence was irrefutable, that denials like the one he'd just heard had almost become meaningless. The caretaker must have been smouldering for years, blaming the priests. Of course, that didn't mean the man had the capacity to kill. Most people, no matter how far they were provoked, couldn't kill easily, the idea that a life was sacrosanct too deeply embedded. But there were others who only needed the slightest provocation. Where Edward Wilson fitted on the scale, he wasn't sure.

10

Billy Liddle stood on the wharf shivering, his thin T-shirt rippling like a sail, offering scant protection against the wind, whose cold talons riffled their way through his lank hair. At that moment, he felt even the wind was a force against him, a mischievous devil mocking him for his delusions. But the cold wind rampaging inland from the North Sea was really an inconsequential discomfort when there were worse things to worry about. In spite of his efforts to deny it, an awful prescience was undermining the sanguine outlook which normally accompanied him through life.

Pike had summoned him to this bleak place. The two gorillas flanking him, coat collars turned up so that their necks seemed even thicker, had arrived at his bedsit half an hour earlier. They told him they had orders to take him to the boss. When he'd tried to wheedle a reason from them, they'd remained uncommunicative, stone-faced. His only smidgeon of comfort was that, in the past, he'd been summoned unceremoniously when the gangster had a job for him. But it had never been this late at night, never to a place that felt like the world's end. He couldn't help fearing the worst.

Two bright circles, like the eyes of a huge animal hunting in the depths of night, suddenly appeared in the distance. A car was heading for the wharf. Soon Billy heard the soft purring of its engine, saw the vehicle's sleek silhouette gliding up to the warehouse in front of him, where it halted. Two men emerged from the car, opened the warehouse doors. One of the men beckoned the car forward and it disappeared into the cavernous darkness like an animal into its lair, not even a flicker of headlights to be seen. The men who'd opened up followed the car inside. One of the gorillas flanking Billy tapped his shoulder.

'On you go, Billy lad,' he said, smiling. 'You'll get warm soon enough in there.'

Billy bit down hard on his bottom lip. Once he entered those doors, he knew he'd be as helpless as a leaf in a tsunami, no chance of running. All he had ever possessed in this world were his wits and his cunning, but Pike was more than his match in those departments. He glanced at the river he'd known all his life, thought about making a break for it, diving into the water, striking out for the far bank, then running until he could run no more, never looking back. But the thought had no substance behind it; he just couldn't do it. The only life he knew was here and old habits died hard. He'd been in deep holes before, dug himself out. Anyway, maybe he was being unduly pessimistic and Pike didn't know anything. Perhaps this creepy place was making him imagine things were worse than they really were. Buoying himself with that thought, he started forward, walking between the two men, his bowed legs and diminutive stature reminiscent of a monkey.

As they entered, the car's interior light flickered into life. One of the gorillas pushed Billy forward. Simultaneously, the warehouse doors closed with a noise like the clash of shields that made him flinch. A shape emerged from the car. Again, he was pushed from behind and he dragged his legs forward as though he was wading through mud. He was a yard away from the bonnet when the headlights came on, their glare momentarily blinding him. By the time he could focus again, a shape had stepped in front of the headlights, a shape he recognized as Pike's.

The gangster folded his arms, leaned his backside on the bonnet. Billy couldn't make out his face but even in this poor light there was an aura about him sufficient to bring the taste of bile surging up from his gullet.

'Do you believe in God, Billy?' the gangster's voice boomed out.

Billy was puzzled; couldn't see the relevance. The only thing he knew for sure was Pike hadn't suddenly got religion, hadn't brought him here in the dark to try to convert him.

'Don't think about it much,' he said warily.

'So it won't upset you that a priest was stabbed to death in Middlesbrough last night?'

Billy didn't know how to answer that one. What did Pike want him to say? He saw a glimmer of hope, though. Maybe this was work related and Pike wanted him to find out something about this priest.

'Wonder what that priest was thinking,' Pike continued, 'when he saw that knife coming at him, felt the pain. Did he lose his faith in those last moments? Did he feel let down . . . by God . . . or by the human beings he'd devoted his life to saving?'

Billy couldn't figure what Pike was getting at, all that religious mumbo-jumbo. Could it be he was losing it? It was weird not being able to see the gangster's face properly, having to judge his mood by his voice. He relied on reading people, adjusting his reactions to whatever he perceived the other person wanted from him, becoming as close as possible to a mirror of that person's thoughts. But if he couldn't see a person's face . . . his eyes . . .

'Why are you asking me, boss?' he mumbled eventually, hoping the evasion wouldn't offend Pike.

'Faith, Billy!' Pike's voice had risen an octave, making Billy jump. 'That's what me and that priest had in common, see. He put his faith in the divine, I put mine in the people who work for me.' He sighed. 'It hurts me when one of my sheep goes astray, Billy. It challenges the order in my world.'

A muffled noise came from the void of darkness behind Billy, one of the gorillas stifling a snigger. Billy couldn't see anything funny. Pike was playing a game here. What was he trying to imply with all that rubbish about the priest? Did he know about McIntyre or not? How should he react? In the end, he decided there was only one way to go.

'Nobody would betray you. Everybody knows you're the man.'

'One denial,' Pike said, his voice sharp now.

Billy swayed as though he'd been punched. His breathing accelerated. Pike knew about him. There could be no doubt about it. The gangster had just been toying with him so far. He was on a tightrope, unfathomable darkness on either side, only a matter of time before he took the long drop into oblivion, unless he could talk his way out.

'I . . . wouldn't . . . '

Pike hissed, 'That's two denials, Billy! One more makes three. You know what that means. The cockerel will crow and Billy will go.'

Billy felt the weight of his fear pressing down on him. Just for a moment, his mind travelled beyond the warehouse, skimmed across the river, flew northward. Why hadn't he taken his chance with the river? All he could do now was grovel though he didn't hold out much hope that would do any good.

'I'm sorry,' he moaned, sounding pathetic even to himself.

'You were seen getting into his car, Billy. You took me for a fool but all the time I was talking to McIntyre I could smell you in that back seat.'

'It wasn't about you, boss. I wouldn't . . . it was . . . something else . . . '

Pike wasn't listening. His voice boomed out.

'Three times denied, then the cock crowed three times. Remember, Billy. Well, I don't need a cockerel 'cos I got little birdies all over the place tweeting in my ears soon as anyone betrays me.'

Billy knew then he was finished; Pike was

going to punish him for sure. Everybody hated grasses. The gangster couldn't afford to be merciful even if it was in his make-up, which Billy knew it wasn't. His people needed to know what would happen to them if they transgressed, needed to fear his wrath. Perversely, that was what had made Billy convince himself that he was immune; nobody would suspect a weakling like him would have the bottle to snitch on the main man. That conceit had led to small betrayals. But then he'd got greedy, gone for the big one. A whimper of despair burst from his lips. How foolish he had been.

'Dispose of this trash!' Pike's voice was as stentorian as a judge's pronouncing sentence and immediately strong hands gripped Billy's arms.

'Gis a chance!' he pleaded. 'Please . . . please.'

He started to wriggle like a fish on a hook, but the hands were too strong, dragged him away, the heels of his cheap trainers trailing on the ground. Pike had already turned away and Billy heard him call over his shoulder.

'Make it look good!'

11

Edward Wilson, the caretaker, had given McIntyre food for thought. He'd made plain his feelings towards priests and the hurt inside him, which would probably never go away until the day he died, was palpable. But why, if he'd done the deed, would he give the police a motive and put himself right in the frame? There was something in the way he'd asserted his innocence that gave the detective a gut feeling he was telling the truth, that he had no involvement. It could be a double bluff, of course it could, but the man didn't strike McIntyre as being that cunning.

His concentration on that matter was disturbed as his difficulties with Kate broke into his thought processes. Her belief that he lacked feeling and compassion hurt him. If that's how she saw him, perhaps he should just forget about her and move on. But her behaviour was mystifying, seemed out of character, and deep down he knew he wasn't ready to give up on her. Probably it was a blessing this case was going to keep him busy so that he wouldn't have time to brood about her.

Half an hour after he'd interviewed the caretaker, he was informed John Bright, the lecturer, had arrived in the building. He cleared his mind of personal matters and waited.

The man who entered was thirty-five years old. As he stared at McIntyre, his body language, especially the arrogant, upward tilt of his chin, seemed to convey he considered it demeaning to be summoned by a person whom he considered his inferior. His dark pin-striped suit, grey waistcoat and polka-dot tie would have been an affectation for a fifty-year-old, never mind a person of his age. Straight off, McIntyre tagged him as striving for an image, a gravitas he lacked. To cut the mustard he would have needed more grey hair, more of a lived-in face than his rather bland boyish features portrayed. In spite of his hackles rising, in a perfunctory show of manners McIntyre lifted himself out of his chair and offered his hand to the lecturer, who limply shook it as though it could be contaminated and he thought he might catch a plague.

'I'm John Bright,' he said, in a condescending tone, 'and you are . . . ?'

McIntyre couldn't help himself. 'Not so bright, myself, but trying hard.'

Bright's features froze. People must have

joked about his name before and he gave the impression he thought the comment puerile.

'Sorry about that,' the detective said, not meaning it. 'Working long hours on murder cases sometimes gets to me and a bit of frivolity helps lighten the mood. I'm DI McIntyre, senior investigating officer. Please be seated. I've a few more questions for you.'

Hitching his trousers at the knees to maintain the creases, Bright sat down and met the detective's gaze.

'Dreadful business. Quite dreadful. A young man with most of his life ahead of him snuffed out like that. A priest as well.'

McIntyre nodded agreement, pleased to see there might be humanity beneath that austere appearance after all. He flicked through papers on his desk.

'I have here the statement you made last night, Mr Bright. Bear with me, please, while I run through the salient points. First off, the classes cleared off at 8.30 p.m. and nobody lingered in the building. You saw the priest in his room at that time.'

Bright nodded. 'Correct.'

'You tidied your classroom, left at 9 p.m., saw the priest in his classroom, called goodnight and he responded in kind. You used the lift, waved to one of the cleaners on the bottom floor as you exited the building.'

'Perfectly correct.'

'And there's nothing you'd change, or add to that.'

Expecting no more than a curt affirmation, McIntyre was ready to move on. He was surprised when there was no answer and looked sharply at the lecturer, who dropped his eyes and brushed his lapel with his fingers.

'Mr Bright?'

Eyelids fluttering like a coy girl's, he looked directly at the detective.

'I'm afraid I'm rather embarrassed . . . can only think that monstrous act disturbed my equanimity more than I thought.' He gave a little shiver and gazed over McIntyre's head. 'To think if I'd stayed longer I might have been the recipient of that foul act. Who knows about fate, Inspector, when small matters of timing can affect our lives so much?'

McIntyre had no time for philosophic meandering. 'Mr Bright! What is it you have to tell me? Is there something else or not?'

The lecturer squeezed his eyes shut, opened them again, nodded.

'Last night, as I struggled for the balm of sleep, in my mind's eye I saw myself leaving my classroom, heard myself calling good-night, watched myself moving down the corridor, pressing the lift button.' He paused,

94

looked vague. 'Funny, isn't it, the intricacy of the mind . . . what the subconscious absorbs and recalls later.'

McIntyre prayed for patience. The man was obviously incapable of simple answers, circumlocution his preferred style. He probably thought he sounded clever to his students while he bored them to death. Well, his students had to endure it but he didn't, not when he was trying to get to the heart of a murder. He immediately cut to the chase.

'With respect, you're not in the lecture room now, Mr Bright. I need facts only. Please get to the point.'

Bright sat back stiffly and scowled at the detective, whose response was to lift an enquiring eyebrow.

'I am sure,' Bright continued sulkily, 'that as I was stepping into the lift I saw a blonde lady standing on the flight of stairs. Her back was turned to me and she was looking out of the window. It was the merest glimpse, which is probably why I didn't recall this until in repose.' He shrugged his shoulders. 'Most likely the shock of Father Riley's murder affected my mental recall.'

McIntyre fell silent. This could be progress because it placed the blonde woman near the murder scene. As for the lecturer's apparent memory lapse, it was plausible; witnesses often recalled things after the event, sometimes were even convinced they'd remembered something only to find they'd imagined it.

'So, does your memory extend to being able to describe this woman for me?'

Bright stroked his chin thoughtfully. 'Her hair was down to her shoulders and she was dressed in black. That's all I recall. She was more of a fleeting shadow at the edge of my vision than flesh and blood, Inspector.' He paused, drew breath. 'Do you think she was the murderer . . . or rather the murderess?'

'It's possible. All I can say is what you've told me is helpful. Have no fear we'll be looking into it.'

Bright gave a tight smile, obviously thinking that concluded matters, and started to rise.

McIntyre held up a hand. 'I have more questions. We're not finished yet.'

Bright gave a supercilious grin, sat down again and twiddled his thumbs, making it clear he was indulging the detective.

McIntyre changed tack. 'How well did you know the victim?'

'Not very. He taught history, a passion of his. I taught literature. We did chat occasionally but he was part-time hours, you see, while I am employed full-time by the university.'

'I don't suppose he gave you any hint that

he had enemies . . . or that anything was troubling him?'

Bright tilted his head again in that haughty manner of his that annoyed McIntyre.

'A priest would hardly confide in a lay person such as myself. It would be the other way round, don't you think?'

McIntyre's hackles rose but he forced a smile. 'A simple yes or no would suffice, Mr Bright, but I'll take it that's a negative. Now, is there anything at all you can tell me about him?'

Bright brushed at his coat collar before he answered. 'Well, he didn't like my atheism. We did argue about that. I like to think I was cool and analytical while he was . . . emotional. Always a sign one is losing a debate. In fact, I thought he protested too much when we engaged in that particular argument.'

'Meaning what exactly?'

'I think he was having doubts about his calling, like a soldier making a last frenzied stand for a cause he no longer has belief in but is unwilling to abandon because he has known it so long.'

McIntyre pondered the value of this amateur psychology. He imagined the real reason the priest became over emotional was because Bright's pompous manner got right up his nose.

'Thanks for that,' he said. 'Anything else?'

Bright stroked his chin. 'Did you know he spent time with prisoners? During our little talks, in order to illustrate the power of religion, he referred to converting convicts. Far be it from me to tell you your job, but that seems an avenue worth exploring. If one chooses to lie down with wolves. Need I say more? One of those criminals . . . '

The amateur psychologist had become amateur sleuth now. Was there no end to his talents? But McIntyre had to concede this was information he couldn't ignore.

'Well, thanks again,' he said. 'I think we can wind this up now.'

Bright rose, unopposed this time, stood straight backed, and let his gaze linger on the detective who, conscious he was under scrutiny, remained silent. This fellow wasn't short of words. If he had anything to say, he wouldn't be able to stop himself. Finally, it came out.

'I am not so naïve, Inspector McIntyre, as to believe I am not regarded as a suspect. It seems apparent that, apart from the killer, I was the last to see the priest alive and the window of opportunity for the murderer following my departure must have been very small.'

McIntyre slumped back in his chair and

audibly exhaled. 'Oh, you're in the frame all right but I shouldn't worry too much.'

A shadow of perplexion flitted across the lecturer's face. 'Really?'

'Brian Clough, Mr Bright. Local lad, brought up in Grove Hill, became a famous football manager. He said it only takes a second to score a goal.'

Bright looked at the detective as though he'd descended from another planet. He stuck out his bottom lip like a frustrated child.

'I don't see . . . '

McIntyre enlightened him. 'It only takes a second to stab someone, a second to die. Whoever did it could have been up and down those stairs in a jiffy. So while you're not out of the frame, you're far from exclusively in it.'

Bright retracted the lip. 'I see . . . but it does feel strange . . . being a suspect. Your colleagues asked so many questions.'

'Par for the course,' McIntyre told him. 'If you're not guilty, don't worry.'

Bright clearly didn't like that curt rejoinder, seemed lost for words for once. With a peeved expression, he nodded his head, turned, flounced to the door and exited without another word.

When he was gone, McIntyre leaned back and sighed long and deep. He considered the man conceited and insecure and pitied the students in his charge. If he was right in his assessment of him, he'd be too wrapped up in himself and his academic world to adjust to the level of those he taught, communicate at the level required. His suggestion that the priest was undergoing a spiritual crisis and the implication that one of his prison converts could have been the murderer might have some truth and needed scrutiny. Resurrecting the blonde on the stairs could, of course, be an attempt to divert the inquiry into blind alleys, cover up his own guilt. All roads were open at this point and it was interesting that Wilson and Bright had both been at pains to point out they were in the frame. At this stage, he wasn't prepared to dismiss the possibility that either could have done it.

12

Bill Clancy hadn't been near the The Fox public house in years but it hadn't changed. The unprepossessing frontage was an anachronism, more suited to the age of sawdust floors and spittoons. It was part of his past and, as he stood there on the pavement, part of him, remembering the better life he'd found, wanted to walk away. But that better life lay in ruins and he was resolved to exorcise it, go back to his old life as though nothing had intervened, find out who had set him up for the prison sentence that had sent his life spiralling out of control. Steeling himself, he pushed the door open; its creaking hinge seemed to protest that this was an unwise move, that he was opening a Pandora's box.

Clancy's eyes swept a lounge so dimly lit a misty gloom seemed to pervade every nook and cranny. He estimated around fifteen men were sitting at the tables, beer glasses in front of them. Almost as one they turned inquisitive faces in his direction, weighing him up as though he was a member of an alien species who'd wandered onto their preserve. Moving towards the bar, he noted the door on the far side of the room, a solitary woman sitting close to it, her face half hidden in shadow.

A bullet-headed barman leaned on the bar, studying the infiltrator, his palms flat on the beer-soaked surface. Clancy noticed the amused twinkle in his eyes. He was sure the guy was thinking a bit of fun was in prospect, something to relieve his boredom.

'Can you do me a half shandy?' he asked politely.

The barman scratched stubble on his chin and smiled to himself as though he thought the newcomer a child who needed indulging.

'A shandy?' he chortled, with an air of mystification. 'A half shandy? Long time since I poured one of those, mate. The men in here drink pints or shorts.'

The stress he laid on the word men was deliberate, clearly designed to let Clancy know he was out of his depth here.

'Then I guess I'm just a half pint who never grew into a proper man, eh!'

Though the words were softly spoken, he accompanied them with a stare he hadn't used since prison. It brought instant confusion to the barman's face. He looked Clancy up and down, reassessing him, then, with a surly shrug of his shoulders, began to make up the shandy he'd asked for.

'I'm looking for someone,' Clancy said, after a moment. 'I'm sure you'll know everybody who comes in, even the half pints.'

The barman sniffed and wiped his nose on the bar towel. 'Someone, you say. Everyone's someone, aren't they, mate? Name the geezer.'

Clancy was about to reply when he noticed the barman's attention drift over his shoulder. He half turned to find the source of his distraction was five men who'd come up behind him. They were all in their mid twenties, short-sleeved shirts clinging to their bodies, the intention to demonstrate their muscles. Clancy knew trouble when he saw it and there was nothing about them to suggest this wasn't it.

He turned back to the barman, beckoned him to come nearer. The man leaned towards him and he spoke loud enough so the five would hear.

'Young people today have no manners, can't mind their own business, so I'll whisper that name in your ear.'

A voice behind responded instantly. 'This is a private room, mate, entry by invitation only. Think you'd better run along.'

Clancy turned around. One of the gang stepped closer, thumbs hooked in his trouser pockets, head tilted to one side, affecting nonchalance.

'I didn't see any signs,' Clancy told him, 'but in any case I'm an old member . . . should probably be an honorary member, truth be told.' He turned his back on the younger man, addressing the barman. 'Now let me give you that name.'

He'd hardly spoken the words when he felt a hand on his shoulder. With that intrusion, like a sudden blast of heat, a fury came upon him. He spun around, vaguely conscious that the seed of his rage had been lurking deep within him since he'd lost his wife and child, had only needed an excuse to burgeon. It wasn't unfamiliar, that rage; it had just been a long time absent. The younger man recognized it and for a fraction of a second seemed unnerved but, with plenty of back-up, he quickly recovered and stepped so close Clancy could smell the beer on his breath.

'You're out of here, shandy man,' he said.

Clancy read what was coming from the movement of his neck muscles and moved his head aside so the attempted head butt only grazed his temple. Now the rage exploded into action. Four straight jabs landed on his tormentor's face and a vacant look came into his eyes. Like a novice skater on ice, he tottered, then went down. His friends caught him just before he hit the floor; they dragged him to a chair, blood pouring from his broken nose. Clancy could hear his own sharp breathing, feel his heart thudding as though someone was pounding at him from inside. But he felt no fear. His rage hadn't subsided and it demanded more freedom after being cooped up so long. Let the others come at him. What did he care any more?

The damaged leader slumped back in the chair, pointed at him, muttered commands distorted by his ruined nose. His four mates needed no translation, rushed at him with flailing arms and flying boots. Clancy knew he had to keep his back against the bar, stay on his feet or he was done for. He managed to knock one out with his first punch but the others renewed their efforts and his rage wasn't enough to sustain him against the superior number. Knees buckling, he went down, lay on the floor, exhausted. Numb in mind and body, he waited for what must surely come. A boot drove into his rib cage and he gritted his teeth, anticipating more. Then, as though from miles away, he heard the sound of a door slamming, someone shouting, the noises echoing like hammer blows in his sore head. No more blows came. He couldn't understand why not. He heard footsteps resounding on the wooden floor.

They came closer, halted near where he lay. A voice he vaguely recognized penetrated his dulled brain.

'What's this?'

'He wouldn't leave, boss,' someone said. 'Barry tried to nut him and took a beating so we all piled in.'

'Said he was here looking for someone,' the barman chipped in. 'Cheeky with it.'

'Turn him over,' that familiar voice ordered, 'and we'll ask him . . . if he can talk.'

Rough hands turned Clancy onto his back. Blood obscuring his vision, he looked up and even through the red mist recognized the face leaning over him, knew from the smile that recognition was mutual.

'Miss the old place too much, did you, Sam?' Pike said. 'Tried to resist its charms but in the end you came slumming, eh!'

Clancy used his elbows to prop himself up. 'Heard you still liked to hang out here,' he grunted, spitting out a tooth. 'Came looking for you but the boys were . . . disrespectful.'

Pike turned to the men who were standing around them in a circle. 'Get him cleaned up, then bring him to the office. And next time make sure you know who you're taking on. This fella and me have history.'

Fifteen minutes later Clancy limped into Pike's office, hurting, but not as damaged as he could have been. The room hadn't altered much; contained only a desk, filing cabinet and a few chairs. Pike was sitting behind the desk. He pointed to a chair. Clancy lowered himself into it.

'Keeps my feet on the ground, this pit does,' Pike said. 'Reminds me of where I started from. When I leave here, I appreciate what I've got.' He pointed to a filing cabinet. 'Stuff in there, all legit. Nothing the bizzies can hold against me when they raid the place.'

'Sentimental about where you started from, eh?' Clancy said.

Pike smiled, his expensive white teeth gleaming. 'Talking of sentiment, is that what this is? Sam Clancy wandering down memory lane, getting his rose-tinted glasses broken into little pieces.' He paused, his little eyes more intense. 'Or, perchance, as you said, did you come looking for me?'

Clancy nodded. 'Looking for you.'

'After all this time? Why not when you got out of prison?' Pike paused, a slyness in his eyes. 'Rumour had it you got married, got religion, then . . . something happened, didn't it?'

'Rumour had it right, but the world turns,' Clancy said, not wishing to discuss his tragedy with this man. 'I want . . . need

. . . my old life back. That's what brought me here . . . to you.'

Pike studied him through his piggy eyes. Clancy knew he was weighing him, wondering whether he had an ulterior motive.

'You mean you want to return to a life of crime?'

Clancy shrugged. 'Needs must. Lost a job I detested but stuck at for my family's sake. Not much chance of anything decent out there for an ex con. Thought you might need someone.'

Pike linked his fingers, leaned forward, pursed his lips, thinking it over. He reminded Clancy of a fat Buddha, the difference being this one had greasy hair and no interest in vows of poverty or the sanctity of life.

'Judging by the mess you made of the silly boy out there,' he said, eventually, 'you can still handle yourself. But the rough stuff was never your thing, was it?'

Clancy shook his head. 'Only when provoked.'

'So a driving job would be best,' the gangster said. 'Making deliveries, some legit, others not. Won't pay much, but if you draw social security and work for me you'll be better off than the average . . . ' Pike hesitated. 'We'll need to be careful, though. Don't want you caught like before.'

Clancy grinned sardonically, said with slow deliberation, 'You haven't forgotten I was set up.'

'I remember,' Pike told him, his face expressionless. 'The bizzies, wasn't it? That's what I heard anyway! But that's past, water under the bridge. So what do you think of my offer?'

'Grateful for anything,' Clancy told him. 'A man's got to earn.'

A silence followed, a tense silence. Clancy realized Pike wasn't too sure of him in spite of employing him and decided he'd try to reassure the gangster.

'This will be a new start for me,' he said. 'Dwelling on the past just eats a person up inside. Prison taught me that. Saw it happen too often to men who couldn't let go.'

'Wise man,' Pike said. 'The strong live without regret. Give me your number. I'll ring when I need you.'

Clancy picked up the pen and paper Pike pushed towards him, wrote his telephone number down and handed it to the gangster. They shook hands, then Pike took out his wallet and laid five £20 notes on the desk.

'Call it a transfer fee,' he said, when Clancy hesitated.

Clancy picked the notes up, did his best to look grateful. 'You won't regret taking me on, I promise.'

Pike waved a hand in the air. 'Need men like you. These youngsters are a different breed. Got everything too easy. Not like us.'

Clancy was aware of the eyes following him as he crossed the lounge, felt waves of hostility, like a psychic force coming at him, from those he'd fought. It reminded him of a time he'd been caught up in a prison riot, hostility vibrating in the air. It was a relief to step outside, drag the fresh air into his lungs. As he walked away, he mused that, though Pike had appeared to accept him back, for sure he would be watching his every move and a slip-up on his part would be fatal.

13

The woman sat in the chair not long vacated by Clancy, Pike eyeing her in a proprietorial manner as he sipped from a glass of whisky.

'You saved your boyfriend from a worse beating,' he grunted with a sneer. 'If you hadn't fetched me in time, they'd have beaten hell out of him.'

Reluctant to show her interest, yet feeling compelled, the woman shrugged and, as nonchalantly as she could manage, asked, 'What did he want?'

Pike licked whisky from the sides of his mouth, the lizard-like movement of his tongue disgusting her. 'He wanted me to give him a job.'

Aware he was watching her like a cat ready to pounce, she remained poker-faced, showed him nothing of her feelings.

'So you gave him a job, did you?'

'Course I did. I'm generous to old friends. Look at you, free-loading off me all these years.'

Once again, she didn't bite. She wasn't in the mood for his games, especially when he was drinking. If she spoke out of turn he wouldn't forget and, now or later, she'd pay for it.

Pike angled his head to the side, smiled so all his teeth were showing, and looked at her as though she was a cute baby who had touched a paternal instinct in him. But it was just part of his act. Both of them knew it.

'Wasn't there even a flutter in that heart of yours, my dear, when you saw your old flame?'

She threw him a look of disdain. 'We weren't much more than kids, Tony. It's so far back it could have been another lifetime. You came along and — '

'Ah, the inconstancy of the human heart,' Pike mocked as she ran out of words. 'It settles but only for a while . . . like a butterfly in clover . . . then moves on. Makes me think you might not really love me unto eternity, dearest.'

She wanted to come back at him, meet sarcasm with sarcasm. But hard-earned experience told her it would be unwise and this wasn't the moment.

Clearly annoyed because he'd failed to provoke a reaction, his mood suddenly grew darker, his voice more vicious.

'State of you these days, maybe he won't even recognize you.'

He wanted to make her feel small and

worthless but she was accustomed to that, inured to his put-downs so that they no longer stung the way they once had. In spite of years of abusing her body, she knew she wasn't that bad, guessed it was a case of good genes overcoming her lifestyle. But for how long? A day would come . . .

'Possibly he won't recognize me. Time changes us all, one way or another.'

Pike pointed a finger. 'Either way, I want you to speak to him, get him to trust you. Find out if he's genuine coming back here.'

'Why would he confide in me?'

Pike smiled. 'Because in our short reac-quaintance he struck me as a haunted man with nothing he really cares about. A man like that has nothing to lose and that can be dangerous. Women are good listeners and maybe he might be a little sentimental about his old amour, all those romantic nights sitting on the garden wall eating fish and chips with you, admiring the view of the steelworks.'

'There's no chance he'll open up to me. I let him down.'

'Just you remember which side your bread is buttered and do as you're told,' Pike snapped. 'Now leave me alone and on your way out send in that punk, Barry.'

She didn't need telling twice, rose quickly

and made for the door, relieved to be out of there, though her relief was tempered by a feeling that Sam Clancy's return was a portent that meant her life would change, and whether for the better or worse, she couldn't be sure.

14

Like a shamefaced schoolboy dabbing at his nose with a handkerchief, Barry stood before Pike, bloodstains covering his shirt. He did his best but failed to hide the pain his broken nose and bruises were causing him. Pike, amused at his discomfort, just smirked.

'So young! So much to learn,' the gangster opined, shaking his head sadly. 'For example, you should never take an unnecessary risk or you might just end up maimed . . . or dead . . . all for nothing.'

'We put him down, boss,' Barry grunted, the effort inducing a fresh spurt of blood from one nostril which he wiped on his sleeve.

'Big deal, sonny. Rest of your life, every time you look at that beak you'll think about him. Know your enemy, kidda, before you take him on.'

'I'll remember that, boss.'

Pike cocked a doubtful eyebrow. 'His name's Sam Clancy and he's going to work for me.'

Barry frowned his displeasure. This was rubbing salt in his wounds. Having the man who'd bust his nose around would be a constant reminder of his folly. But he knew better than to protest.

'You must trust this guy, boss.'

'We go back,' Pike said. 'He'll be an asset . . . if he's genuine.'

'If he's genuine?' Barry picked up on that quickly enough, his voice distorted by the blood in his nasal passages. 'Bud . . . bud . . . you just said no unnecessary risks.'

Pike nodded. 'That's right, but someone you have doubts about, keep them close, where you can see them . . . anticipate the worst thing. I don't trust him, not yet, so I want you and the lads to watch him, report anything suspicious.'

Barry tried a smile but his pain trans-formed the attempt into a wince.

'My pleasure, boss.'

Pike pointed a stubby finger at his own pudgy nose.

'You're like me, kidda. You weren't ever going to be a looker, so forget what he did to your beak. Don't push him because of what he did to you. Just observe. Believe me, he'll know if you try too hard.'

'You want me to be friendly?'

'You got it. Friendly it is.'

'You're a clever man, boss.'

Pike preened. 'Call me streetwise, kidda.

Better that than being educated. Learned my lessons the hard way, not from some book. Now you run along to A and E, sort out that broken beak.'

15

McIntyre admired the treelined avenue. He was in Acklam, a part of Middlesbrough where the houses were old but stately, with spacious, well-kept gardens. It was a world away from Grove Hill; here people lived their lives in enviable peace, except for an occasional burglar encroaching on their ordered lives. He'd parked in front of Bishop Wright's house. The dignitary had already been informed of Father Riley's death and he was expecting this visit. Back at headquarters, the team were busy delving into the suspects' backgrounds. McIntyre was here to learn more about the murdered priest.

A woman answered when he rang the bell. Her brown hair was tied back close to her scalp, the style serving to emphasize hollow cheeks untouched by make-up. Her plain grey cardigan was a size too big and McIntyre had the impression this was a woman who didn't care too much for her personal appearance. She didn't proffer a smile, instead greeted him with a look so cold and severe it could have turned water to ice and left little doubt he wasn't welcome. McIntyre took the initiative, the coolness in his voice matching her demeanour.

'I'm Detective Inspector McIntyre. The bishop is expecting me.'

With a curt nod, she opened the door wide and, avoiding his gaze, stood aside. He found himself entering a long hall, its panelled walls adorned with religious paintings.

As she brushed past him, she spoke with what sounded to him like resigned languor. 'Second door on the right. Follow me.'

She led him into a small room that reminded him of a doctor's waiting room he'd known as a boy, except it had a desk, which the woman scuttled behind as though she needed to put a barrier between them as swiftly as possible. From there, she waved a hand dismissively.

'Be seated. You will need to wait.'

Confused and not a little intrigued by her condescending manner, he sat on a hard chair, the only one available. The woman didn't look at him, started examining papers on her desk, though he had the feeling she wasn't really concentrating, merely avoiding having to communicate. Did she have a thing about policemen, he wondered, or was it something specifically to do with him? Though she hadn't introduced herself, he presumed she was the bishop's secretary.

McIntyre felt his patience draining away with each passing moment. He didn't like to be kept waiting when he was investigating a murder. Eventually, he spoke up, not unpleasantly.

'You are the bishop's secretary, aren't you?'

'Yes, I am,' she answered, not looking up.

'In that case, it would probably save time for us both if you gave me a list of the members of the congregation at St Peter's.'

Her response was to stare vaguely in his direction, as though she was so preoccupied she had only half heard. But she must have done, because just as he was about to repeat himself, she found her voice.

'You will have to have the bishop's permission for that.'

It wasn't the words that irked him so much as her sharp manner, as though she was speaking to a child who was annoying her. With great difficulty, he kept his voice level.

'Do you know why I'm here?'

'I presume you're here because Father Riley has been murdered,' she said, the lack of emotion in her voice, the blank look in her eyes, reinforcing his first impression that this woman was a cold fish, a poor advert for Christian charity indeed.

'Well, then,' he said, his stare burning. 'I'm telling you I need that list and don't require anyone's permission ... so get it ready ... please. Are we clear?'

Given her previous demeanour, he expected an argument, but she didn't give him one. Instead, she rose languidly and opened the cabinet. While she was fiddling through the files, the door opened and a grey-haired gentleman with a girth that arrived before the rest of him and bespoke a multitude of good dinners ambled in. He offered the detective his hand, announcing himself in a voice that boomed unnecessarily loud for the small room.

'I'm Bishop Wright, Officer. You must be Inspector ... McIntyre. Sorry you had to wait. Let's go to my office where it's more comfortable, shall we?'

As they moved out of the room, McIntyre glanced back at the woman and spoke loud enough so the bishop would hear.

'You will have that list ready for me when I leave, won't you?'

The bishop's room was as spacious as his secretary's room was cramped. Bookshelves stretching to the ceiling covered an entire wall, religious and landscape paintings adorned the other walls. A large desk with a designer curve that made the detective wonder whether it was custom built to accommodate the bishop's swollen stomach stood in front of a bay window which overlooked a verdant garden. The bishop, seating himself in one of three leather armchairs, invited the detective to take his pick from the other two.

When they had both sunk into the depths of the chairs, clasping his hands together on the upper slopes of his stomach, the bishop spoke.

'Poor Father Riley. It's tragic, simply tragic. I can hardly believe it. So young, so much still to offer.'

McIntyre concurred that indeed it was tragic, then got down to business.

'As I already informed you, he was stabbed twice. We haven't arrested anyone yet. If you could fill in a bit of his background that would be useful at this stage.'

'Of course, Inspector. What, in particular, would you like me to address? Can you be specific?'

McIntyre leaned back. 'Had he any enemies? Was he involved in any disputations which might have led to acrimony?'

The bishop drew in a wheezy breath, pulled at one of his double chins, pondered the questions, shook his head.

'Nothing of such a magnitude that it could have led to his murder, I can assure you of that.'

'What about the prisoners he worked with? None of them tried to take advantage? They have their ways, believe me, even when they're behind bars.'

'I doubt that very much, Inspector. He was astute, not a naïve man, and he was well aware of the potential dangers from that direction. He would have nipped them in the bud, I'm sure.'

McIntyre hid his disappointment. He'd been hoping to glean a possible motive for the murder from the priest's working life. At the same time, he knew his failure didn't mean there wasn't something. How well did any boss know his employees?

'Nothing provocative in his life, then?' McIntyre mused, as though he was asking himself the question.

The bishop gazed at the detective, his eyes opaque for a moment, as if not sure whether he should voice something he was thinking. Finally, he blew out his cheeks and overcame what had appeared to McIntyre an inhibition.

'If I were to speculate, Detective, there are other valid scenarios peculiar to the life of a priest which you may not have considered and might explain his terrible demise.'

McIntyre frowned. 'Please feel free to speculate, Bishop. What is it they say? Speculate to accumulate.'

The clergyman leaned so far back in his chair that his stomach rose to form a near-perfect dome.

'The office of a priest can arouse peculiar emotions in people, sometimes dark and dangerous emotions, Inspector. By the nature of his calling he is a man apart, a symbol of a way of life. There are those who come to hate religion, and by association its representatives. Such a person could target a priest at random, out of obsessive anger at Christianity itself.'

McIntyre stroked his chin. 'In a nutshell, you're saying it could be a madman who has had no real personal dealings with Father Riley.'

The bishop linked his fingers to form a bridge across the risen dome. 'In my humble opinion, you must consider that.'

The caretaker, Edward Wilson, sprang into McIntyre's mind. He appeared near obsessive in his hatred of priests, whom he blamed for his daughter's death. But his was a more personal obsession than the theory the bishop had put forward, because he did know Father Riley.

'I'll keep what you say in mind, Bishop. Policemen have been murdered for similar motives: hatred for the uniform, what it stood for regardless of the poor man wearing it.'

Bishop Wright smiled benignly. 'It would be better for the Church if the killer were a madman. That would induce public sympathy, you see. On the other hand, if there was anything scandalous involved, well, it would be a blow. Fortunately, I believe Father Riley to be a man of good character, devoid of scandal.'

That speech surprised McIntyre. The body wasn't long cold and the bishop, from whom he would have expected greater sensibility, was already thinking like a politician. His attitude was disrespectful to a dead man. Was the bishop a hypocrite, he wondered, espousing a creed he didn't practise himself? Perhaps he simply lacked self-awareness.

'Could you send me a summary of Father Riley's career, dioceses he's lived and worked in, going back as far as you can?'

The bishop made an expansive gesture with his hands. 'But of course. My secretary, Miss Prebble, will see it's delivered to your headquarters the minute it's compiled.'

'Obliged to you,' McIntyre said and started to rise. 'And by the way, I have already asked your secretary for a list of the members of Father Riley's congregation. However, she seemed a little . . . reluctant to let me have it.'

Like a walrus shuffling along on a beach,

layers of fat wobbling, the bishop manoeuvred his corpulent frame out of the chair.

'She wasn't co-operative, Inspector?' he snapped.

'Perhaps that would be an exaggeration but the list is important, as is the history of Father Riley's career in the Church. So soon as, please.'

'And you shall have it!' The bishop's lower lip protruded like a petulant child's. 'That woman has been acting very strangely of late. I can't imagine what's got into her. She's never had the sunniest disposition but recently it's as though she's lost the ability to smile or converse pleasantly. I will have a word.'

'Probably it's just a phase she's going through,' McIntyre offered.

The bishop trundled out of the room, told McIntyre to wait in the hall and entered the secretary's office. He soon emerged and handed McIntyre the list of names he'd requested.

'Good luck, Inspector,' he said, opening the front door and shaking McIntyre's hand over vigorously. 'I'm sure you'll go gently if you have to question any of our flock.'

McIntyre smiled. 'People are people, Bishop Wright. I treat them as I find them.'

Back in his car, the detective sat a

moment, going over his visit from start to finish. It struck him that, like the lecturer John Bright, the bishop had quite enthusiastically offered theories about the priest's murder. No doubt in their chosen vocations they were accustomed to expressing their views and automatically expected them to carry weight. But, even allowing for that, his intuition told him they were pushing a bit too hard and somehow it didn't sit right with him.

Turning his attention to the list he'd been given, he wasn't too surprised to find Kate's name on it because he knew she attended St Peter's. Perhaps he should kill two birds with one stone, use it as a reason to visit her. It could prove a disastrous move, of course, but he wanted to try to make peace with her. Before he drove off, he decided he'd do it.

16

Evening was beginning to steal the day away as he drove into Done Roaming. He sat a while in the car park, studying Kate's flat. Her lights were on so chances were she was inside. All he had to do was go right up to the door, knock and, when she answered, state his business. Easy as that. But when it came to it, trepidation made him hesitate. Would she consider his visit merely an annoying subterfuge? If she did, he might be blowing whatever chance he had with her out of the water.

As he was struggling with those ambivalent thoughts, the door of the flat opened and Kate appeared, a man in a beanie alongside her. Sliding down in his seat, McIntyre watched her give him a peck on the cheek before he stepped out into the night and she closed the door. As her visitor headed for the exit, the poor light made it difficult to make out his features, but the detective's imagination was certainly stirred by what he'd just seen and it was telling him it was evidence Kate had a boyfriend, that she'd simply needed an excuse, any excuse, to finish with him. He quickly reproached himself for jumping to conclusions. The best thing would be to do what he'd come here to do, and see what developed when he and Kate were face to face. Resolved to take that step, he got out of the car and strode to the building.

Kate answered his third knock, and greeted him in a pleasant enough tone.

'Hello there, Don.'

Like her voice, her facial expression showed no sign of hostility, which encouraged him a mite.

He shuffled his feet, muttering, 'Sorry to disturb you. I'm involved in an investigation, you see, thought you might be able to help — as it happens — coincidentally — otherwise . . . '

The words dried up but she opened the door wider and saved him from his embarrassment.

'Whatever it is, it sounds serious. You'd better come in.'

Slightly bemused, he followed her into the living room and sat in a familiar chair, reminding himself this visit was official and not to get too comfortable. She sat facing him, blue eyes assessing him, and he thought how comfortable they'd been in each other's company. Perhaps he had been deceiving himself all along, though, and she hadn't felt the same way.

'I know what you said about wanting . . . space,' he opened, 'but I think you might be able to help me with this case.'

She wafted a hand in front of her. 'You already said it's an investigation that brings you here. I'm fine with that.'

So far, so good, he thought, wondering whether she'd regretted the quarrel or was simply accommodating him because he'd told her it was business. He had a pang of conscience because there was no denying there were personal reasons behind the visit.

'It's about Father Riley.'

She gave a little shiver. 'I know he's been murdered,' she said. 'So they gave the case to you, did they?'

'For my sins, you might say.'

She frowned. 'But I don't see how I can help.'

McIntyre chose his words carefully, hoping he sounded convincing.

'Your name was on the list of church members. Since I know you, rather than send some other cop I thought it would be easier for you if I came . . . but perhaps I got that wrong.'

'That was very considerate,' she said, with a smile to herself that made him sure she'd rumbled him. 'But, as I said, I don't see what help I can be.'

'Well, you can start by telling me what you thought of the priest?'

She was silent for a moment while she considered his question.

'I didn't know him that well. He was pleasant enough, patient with old people, always willing to help them, especially in spiritual matters. Why anyone would want to kill him is beyond me.'

It was a fairly comprehensive answer, nothing much to tease out of it beyond the mundane. Really there'd be no reason to linger any longer, unless he steered the conversation to matters which had, in truth, drawn him here. Fortunately, Kate rescued an awkward moment.

'This is the second tragedy to hit St Peter's,' she stated. 'Not so long ago Mrs Clancy committed suicide, taking her four-year-old son with her. Now Father Riley's been murdered.'

The detective remembered hearing about the suicide. The mother and son had jumped off the Transporter Bridge, an iconic landmark known throughout the world, but unfortunately a place chosen by a few poor souls who wanted to end their existence.

Katie shook her head sadly. 'There was no

obvious reason for them to take their lives,' she continued. 'Mrs Clancy's husband, poor man, is devastated. His name will probably be on your list. If he's to be interviewed, please be tactful.'

McIntyre took the list from his pocket, unfolded it, looked for the name but couldn't find it.

'There's no Clancy on the list.'

'There's no Samuel Clancy? You're sure of that?'

McIntyre shook his head. 'If he's a church member, he should be here.'

She frowned, gave the matter more consideration. 'It could be whoever drew up the list wanted to protect him. As I mentioned, he's devastated.'

'Protect him!' McIntyre realized he'd raised his voice and softened his tone. 'That would constitute obstructing a murder inquiry. Why would anyone risk that?'

'I wouldn't know but if I had to guess I'd say it's possible someone thought a detective asking questions was the last thing he needed when he was grieving for his wife; that compassion was called for.'

McIntyre remembered the night they'd fallen out. She'd accused him of lacking compassion. Had she used the word again now as a barb to remind him where he stood in her estimation?

'If that's the case, they did themselves and Mr Clancy a disservice; made more work for the police at a time when they're concentrating on a murder.'

He half expected her to bite back at him but she was silent and looking thoughtful. Then, with obvious reluctance, she spoke out again.

'There's another reason why he could have been omitted from your list but I feel my telling you is like hitting a man when he's down.'

'You should tell me, Kate. It could be important.'

With a pained expression, she elaborated, 'Sam Clancy is an ex prisoner whom Father Riley brought into his fold. I suppose his past would make him a suspect so perhaps someone left him off the list as a . . . kindness . . . knowing his state of mind.'

McIntyre couldn't help himself. 'I'll have to join the Church. All this compassion and kindness — sounds like paradise on earth. Let's hope he isn't involved.'

He immediately regretted the comment. Kate already seemed to believe him insensitive and he had probably just reinforced that opinion. Before she had a chance to comment, he continued.

'Thanks for your candour, Kate. Know what you mean about kicking a man when he's down. I'll look into it . . . very tactfully.'

They'd reached a hiatus, a time for him to broach other matters or make his exit. The ensuing silence was uncomfortable, McIntyre knowing what he wanted to say but reluctant to begin. In the end, his courage failed him. She'd said she'd wanted time and maybe he should give her that, let her work it all out herself. With an inward sigh, he rose to his feet.

'You've been a help,' he said dryly. 'Thanks for that.'

Nothing more was said as he made his way into the hall, Kate following him. When he opened the front door a blast of wind burst in, slapped his face like a cold flannel. It felt like a reprimand and he suddenly found his courage. He swung round to face her. If the answer was negative, so be it. Life would go on and he'd know where he stood.

'Look, Kate, did you find someone else? If so, it's OK, but I'd rather know.'

His outburst took her by surprise. Eyes growing wide, cheeks flushing with indignation, she responded vehemently.

'What do you think I am? If there was someone, I would have told you straight.'

He'd seen lying eyes of all kinds in his

time. In her penetrating stare, he saw only that she was telling the truth, that she was angry that he thought she might be a two-timer. Relieved, but feeling foolish, he stood there like an idiot, not knowing what to say. Fortunately, she came to his rescue, her tone more reconciliatory than he expected.

'Look, there's something bad going on in my life and I took it out on you because you were saying things that hit a nerve. It wasn't fair on you. It wasn't like me. I wasn't myself.'

McIntyre had suspected as much, so wasn't too surprised. Why hadn't she confided in him? he wondered.

'You should have told me. Maybe I could have helped. Maybe I still can for all I know.'

His words, meant to comfort her, had the opposite effect, brought fear into her eyes, and he was perplexed. One thing was crystal clear, though. Whatever her problem was, she didn't want to share it with him.

'We could go for a drink . . . s-sometime,' he stammered.

Her silence, that frightened rabbit look on her face, conveyed as forcefully as any words that a drink with him was out of the question. He felt wounded. There was a wall between them and he couldn't understand the reason.

'Give me time, Don. Please . . . I just need

time,' she said eventually.

He felt a flicker of anger. Was she playing games? Her desperate look, the look of a cornered animal who doesn't know which way to turn, told him otherwise and his anger dissipated straightaway and he could only feel sympathy. But if she wasn't prepared to confide in him he'd have to back off, hope she might come around eventually.

'I understand,' he mumbled. 'If you need me . . . You mean a lot to me, you know.'

She gave a faint smile and went quiet. McIntyre hesitated, feeling he'd said enough. Frustrated by what he took to be her obduracy, he opened the door and stepped out.

'Well, you know my number,' he called over his shoulder.

As he walked away, the wind howled in his ear like a child in pain and he could sense her watching him. When he reached his car, he turned to wave, but she had already shut the door and his heart plummeted.

He drove away with mixed emotions, pleased there was a chance but mystified by her behaviour. She'd asked for more time. He'd go along with that but he hoped she would relent and come to him for help. Meanwhile, he had work to do and Sam Clancy needed a closer look.

17

McIntyre's father handed him a mug of steaming coffee. The detective had passed the flat after his meeting with Kate and, feeling guilty, decided to look in. The place was clean and brightly decorated but didn't have the same feel as his home in Wolviston and he felt strange being there; though he had to admit, at his father's age, it hadn't made sense to live in a big house. What had possessed his father to move back to Grove Hill, after being away years, was beyond his son's comprehension. Challenged about it, all he would say was that he wanted to die in the place he was born and bred.

'So, you're well settled,' McIntyre said, studying his father over the top of his mug, thinking he looked healthy enough for his advanced years.

His father sat down with him. 'Can't complain. My old pals are still here. We have history . . . reminisce.'

'Well, my offer still stands. You can come and live with me. My place is big enough.'

The old man shook his head. 'Appreciate that, son, but it wouldn't work. You're never in. I wouldn't see you. Don't you worry, I can manage here.'

McIntyre sipped his coffee. 'The old reprobates you mix with. Do they remember why you left Grove Hill?'

The old man's eyes watered. McIntyre could have cursed himself for bringing that up. Why couldn't he just forget? But he'd said it now; couldn't recall it.

'They don't blame me, if that's what you're thinking. They understand and don't think any less of me.'

McIntyre was quiet for a moment. His mother's death, almost as soon as they'd moved away, Paul's passing only a few years later, had done damage to the living they'd left behind. No matter how hard he tried, he couldn't get rid of the idea that giving in to a bully like Pike had led, albeit indirectly, to his family tragedies. The bitter memories stood like shadows between him and his father to this day.

'Any nearer to catching him?' his father asked.

'Catching who?'

His father lifted his eyebrows. 'You know who I mean. Pike! Who else but him?'

McIntyre turned towards the window. It was dull outside, turning misty. On the opposite rooftop, birds were hunched in a long, sinister-looking line, like a sombre column of infantry awaiting orders. Dark clouds scurried across the sky above them as though they needed to be somewhere in a hurry, no time to waste. How much time had he wasted in his pursuit of Pike? McIntyre wondered.

'Thought I had him here,' he told his father, opening his palm, 'but he slithered away.' Eyes cold, he added, 'There'll be another time. On my brother's grave, there will be.'

His father stared down at the floor, as though he was deep in thought. Then, shaking his head, he looked up at his son, disappointment in his eyes.

'You're obsessed, Don. You'll have to ease up. One way or another sins come home to roost and Pike has a surfeit of sins that will find him out. Try to enjoy your life, son, before it's too late.'

'Is that how you come to terms with . . . ' McIntyre was going to mention Paul's fate but caught himself in time and bowed his head. 'It doesn't work for me,' he muttered. 'Pike's still out there ruining lives and it's true catching him is an obsession with me. How could it be otherwise?'

His father's shoulders slumped forward. A piteous expression crept into his face.

'I'll never come to terms with Paul's death, but I know what goes round comes around. Like I said, don't ruin your life going after Pike.'

McIntyre screwed up his face as though he'd tasted bad food.

'It's taking a long time for justice to come around to him . . . years too long.'

His father grimaced in his chair. 'You still blame me for moving away, don't you? After all this time.'

He didn't want to answer the question. So many times he'd tried to banish the idea that his father had acted in a cowardly fashion but his emotions ran too deep and he couldn't. It kept resurfacing and, in spite of himself, he would give vent to his feelings. Later, he would regret hurting his father.

'You did your best,' he mumbled.

The old man pushed himself out of his chair, turned away from his son and stood by the window. On the roof opposite, the birds took flight in one black line and disappeared into the mist. After what seemed an age, his father turned back to him.

'Before I forget, I had a letter asking me to call in to collect Aunt Violet's personal effects. Wonder whether you could do that for me when you have time?'

McIntyre had first met Kate while visiting

his mother's sister, Violet, who was domiciled in Done Roaming in her latter years. She'd died just before his father had returned to the area.

'Sure,' he said. 'No problem.'

They chatted a little longer, the strain between them easing. As he parted from his father, McIntyre, as he'd known he would, felt a little ashamed. His old man had been a good parent in so many ways. Deep down, he felt gratitude and love for him. Why, then, had those other emotions to keep surfacing and causing so much pain?

18

Sam Clancy sipped his whisky, his second of the night. After years of abstention, he'd returned to the old tempter, could feel the familiar burn, hoped the keen-edged emotions he was trying to banish would at least be anaesthetized for a little while. Remaining in this house wasn't healthy. The cremation of his wife and son's possessions had helped a little, but every room still carried memories that seemed to come floating at him out of the ether, reminding him of what he'd lost, stopping him in his tracks. For sure, leaving would he hard, but the sooner he did it the better if he was to excise the happy years from his life as though they'd never been.

An urgent rapping interrupted his melancholy. He didn't want to answer the door, didn't feel like human company. But the rapping persisted. Finally, he put the glass down, made his way reluctantly down the hall and opened up.

A woman's face loomed at him out of the darkness, conjured a fragment of memory he couldn't clarify. As he stared, a name began to attach itself to her features, though he was sure he must be mistaken, that the booze had fogged his brain to the extent he was imagining this person was someone who had once been part of his life but was surely only a figment.

'Don't you recognize me, Sam?' a plaintive voice complained.

His memory reconciled the voice with the face, giving him a start when he realized she was no delusion. Time had touched her but only with the lightest brush and the girl he'd known, if not so luminous and lissom as in those more innocent days, hadn't changed so much. Wide eyed with surprise, he spoke her name.

'Joan Burton!'

'The same old gal,' she said, facial muscles visibly relaxing.

He stared at her, not speaking, bemused by her appearance on his doorstep. They'd been close once but that closeness had ended when he'd gone to prison. She hadn't bothered to visit or write, so he'd put her out of his mind, telling himself he'd been mistaken about her, that she was shallow, that their relationship hadn't stood the test. All that and much more whirled through his brain. He didn't know what to say and it was she who took the initiative.

'I can guess what you are thinking, Sam,

but I really need to speak to you. It's important or I wouldn't have bothered you.'

Her voice seemed to reach him from afar, crossing time and years. Finally, realizing he was standing there like a zombie, he pulled himself together.

'You'd better come in, then.'

He knew his voice hadn't sounded welcoming but, in truth, did she deserve anything better?

He led her to the living room, made sure she didn't sit in Mary's chair. With every second's passing, her presence felt more and more surreal, as though she'd transcended time as part of his wish to go back to his other life.

'I can tell you don't like me coming here,' she said, when she was seated, 'and I can understand why.' She glanced down at her feet. 'For what it's worth, I'm sorry about what happened to your wife and son.'

He gave the slightest nod of acknowledgement. 'So why are you here, Joan? Why now? What can we possibly have to say to each other?'

He made no attempt to hide the hint of sarcasm in his voice, the subtext that she hadn't bothered when he really needed her.

She gave him a long-suffering look. 'You haven't a clue about what happened back then, have you, Sam?'

'I went to prison. That's what happened. End of the story.'

'You think I gave up on you, don't you?'

'Looked that way to me.'

She pulled nervously at a loose strand of hair. 'I had a good reason.'

'Sure you did. Cost of the bus fare couldn't have helped either.'

'Pike!' Ignoring the jibe, she spat the word out like something foul. 'He was the reason.'

Clancy's lips shaped into a twisted smile. 'I understand. Fell for his good looks and charm. How could you help yourself?'

Disappointment dulled her eyes. 'I've come here with good intentions, to try to make amends,' she said. 'The Sam Clancy I knew back in the day would have done me the courtesy of at least listening before he judged me. But I suppose you judged me long ago and who can blame you, really?'

'Long ago!' He hurled those words back at her. 'Like in another lifetime, you mean. How can you make amends now?'

'If you hadn't revisited the past, if you hadn't gone to The Fox, I wouldn't be here now, Sam. Who do you suppose told Pike his men were beating you?'

Now he remembered the woman in the shadows. It must have been her all along.

Pike's timely intervention wasn't just chance then. He had to concede, reluctantly, he owed her for saving him from a savage beating.

'Appreciated,' he mumbled, as though he could hardly bear to say the word to her. 'But I still don't understand what you're doing here?'

'First,' she said, 'I'll explain some of that ancient history you're so anxious to dismiss. You'll see its relevance and understand why I had to come here . . . unwillingly.'

In spite of himself, she'd piqued his curiosity. But he was still wary because she was connected to Pike and that was enough to arouse suspicion of her motives.

'Fire away. I'm all ears.'

She hesitated, stared at the mantelpiece, and began to fiddle with the buttons on her coat as though they constituted a rosary and she was counting her prayers. Clancy realized she was nervous and started to feel sorry for her because it was clear her trepidation was no act. Finally, she overcame her inhibition.

'Pike stopped me from coming to see you in prison.'

He leaned back, studied her, said doubt-fully, 'The girl I knew back then wouldn't have let anyone stop her doing what she wanted, not even him.'

Her top lip curled upward in disdain.

'You were too naïve to see that he'd been chasing me. I kept him at arm's length and he grew more jealous of you by the day. When you went to prison, he warned me if I made any kind of contact he'd see you suffered inside. I knew he could do it, so I obeyed.' Joan sighed. 'I was devastated, started taking drugs to shut out the pain. My dependency grew. He became my supplier and . . . that's how I became his woman'.

Clancy felt his antipathy towards her start to drain away. All this time he'd believed she'd forsaken him in his hour of need. Even now, he didn't want to accept her version, preferred to think it was a fiction. But the risk she was taking in betraying Pike, her nervous manner, were beginning to convince him.

'Time and time again I was going to run away,' she continued, wringing her hands, 'but I was . . . am . . . dependent on him for my fixes, couldn't find the courage, and let myself drift along until I was lost.' She sighed. 'I'm weak and pathetic, Sam. You don't know what it took to drag myself here tonight.'

Clancy was dumbstruck. She hadn't abandoned him, after all; just the opposite, had sacrificed herself for him and paid a price. He felt ashamed of his hostility.

'I'm so sorry,' he muttered, guilty for misjudging her, then and now.

She gave him a reproving glance. 'Don't you go thinking I came here for pity or sympathy. I should have run away. That's my fault.'

Clancy grimaced as a thought struck him. 'He'll kill you if he finds out you told me.'

'Hear me out,' she said. 'Then you'll know why I've taken that risk. But first tell me why you wanted to be back with Pike? You'd moved on, escaped that kind of life.'

'I've nowhere else to go,' he told her. 'I want my old life back. I tried a different road, believed what a priest told me. It was good for a time and then it all collapsed beneath me. But there is another reason I want to go back. Someone set me up back then and it still rankles. I want to know who it was.'

Lost in bitter memory, he stared at the carpet. When he looked up, he saw Joan was holding back tears.

'That's me,' he said. 'Now you tell me why you've taken this risk?'

Her indecision was palpable. Behind her glassy eyes, he could see her thoughts trading blows.

'You've had enough to deal with,' she mumbled, eyes darting everywhere except at him. 'Maybe my coming here was a mistake. I can only hurt you more.'

'Nothing can hurt me much now,' he told

her. 'Nothing! So just tell me.'

She drew in a breath. 'You always said you were innocent, shouldn't have been put in prison.'

He nodded. 'Yes, and you believed me because you knew how much I hated drugs and didn't want to have anything to do with them.'

'Well, I know for sure you were set up, Sam.'

'I've always been sure I was set up.'

'But you don't know who was responsible.'

'Can't accuse anybody without proof, can you?'

She avoided his stare. He noticed worry lines forming around her mouth, guessed, if she told him, she was stepping over a line which, once crossed, meant danger for her. In a voice so hoarse it seemed to have been dredged up from the depths of her soul, she finally surrendered.

'Pike! It was Pike!'

Clancy didn't show any surprise because he'd always had Pike in mind.

'How do you know this?'

'You were well into your sentence,' she explained, watching his face, trying to gauge his reaction. 'Pike was drinking heavily, in a mood, trying to goad me. That's when he told me he'd planted the drugs in your flat, got the bizzies on to you. I was disgusted, but also terrified, sure he'd kill me now that I knew he was as low as the snitches he claimed he despised. Luckily for me, he'd been so drunk that night he didn't remember anything.'

When she'd finished, her relief was palpable, a burden she'd carried too long fallen from her shoulders. Clancy outwardly remained impassive, though he was churning inside, hearing the truth of his betrayal laid out so starkly.

'Forgive me!' Joan burst out, unsure what he was thinking. 'I should have gone to the police but I was afraid for both of us.'

'Wouldn't have done any good,' Clancy said. 'Your word against his. They'd have laughed in your face and, if Pike got wind of it, he'd have made you suffer.'

After a moment of silence, she said, 'I couldn't let you go back to him without knowing the truth. But now I'm afraid of what you'll do, Sam.'

'He needs to pay for those years he took from me,' he replied with a hard glint in his eye.

Joan gave a sad sigh. 'I hoped you'd walk away. You tasted a better way of life. Why go back now?'

'I should have gone back instead of marrying my wife,' he growled. 'If I had done that she would still be alive.' His eyes clouded over. 'My wife committed suicide, jumped off the Transporter with my little boy. I can only think I failed them and it would have been better if she'd never met me. She was a good person, you see, deserved a better man.'

Joan reached across the space between them, touched his arm in a sympathetic gesture but he pulled away from her.

'You're still in mourning, not thinking straight,' she said gently. 'That's only natural. Give yourself more time.'

He stared at the mantelpiece, at the blank spaces where the photographs had been.

'I wish we could turn back time,' he said plaintively. 'I'll never see them again and the future feels like a desert I have to cross alone without the sustenance every soul needs.' He gave a cruel laugh. 'There was a priest who nearly convinced me that there was an afterlife. Can you believe it?'

'None of us know, Sam.'

'It was just a drug,' he snapped. 'You do know about drugs, what happens when the illusion wears off?'

His immediately regretted his callous words but, even though they hurt her, she didn't relent.

'I know it sounds rich coming from me, but we all need hope, Sam.'

He looked at her scathingly. 'My wife had hope . . . and faith. They weren't enough even for a strong person like her.' He put his head in his hands. 'Did I steal them away from her?'

'Maybe it had nothing to do with you,' she said. 'One thing you can be sure of is that, if she were here now, she wouldn't want you to go back to your old life or to seek revenge.'

Clancy's upper lip rose contemptuously. 'We'll never know about that, will we? Anyway, my mind's made up.'

She opened her mouth to protest but something adamantine in the look he gave her told her it would do no good. He'd drawn down a portcullis to shut her out so she changed her tack.

'I know a policeman, a fair man. He'll help you get Pike . . . lawfully. Think about that before you destroy yourself for someone who's not worth it.'

After that final effort to make him see sense, she rose and walked out of the room. Clancy followed her, his movements lethargic because speaking about his wife and son had drained him emotionally. When they reached the door, he stretched an arm over her shoulder to open it. She turned to face him and he was suddenly struck by how small and vulnerable she looked and he felt ashamed he'd treated her so brusquely when she'd come here with his welfare in mind. Not only that, she'd also put her own life at risk in the process.

'I am grateful, Joan,' he mumbled. 'Don't think I'm not.'

'It's less than I owe you, Sam. I am your friend, you know, no matter what . . . always will be.'

'You're the same good woman I remember,' he said, trying to make up for his earlier coldness.

She blushed the way he remembered she had as a teenager. 'I know what I am. You just be careful which path you take, Sam Clancy.'

He thought he saw a tear, but she'd turned and walked out into the night before he could be sure. Later, as he lay in bed, he replayed their reunion in his mind and had to allow that her parting words had made an impact, raising doubts about the direction he was heading.

19

Harry Drew, the governor of Stockton Prison, was a dirty five-a-side soccer player. McIntyre thought that was because, like many of his own colleagues, he used the game to rid himself of all the frustrations of his job. They played against each other regularly and, in spite of their clashes on the pitch, hostilities had been confined to that arena. That had proved advantageous when he'd asked for the governor's co-operation at short notice.

'I'm grateful,' the DI said from the chair opposite the governor's desk. 'As I told you on the phone, I'm investigating Father Riley's murder and need to talk to his flock here . . . soon as . . . see whether they can help me.'

'It was short notice, Don,' Harry said, adjusting his heavy-framed glasses, his need for which, off the pitch, was often his excuse for his dirty tackles on it. 'But I have arranged interviews with three of his regulars. We'll not advertise your presence. Nobody but those three will know your identity . . . or your business here.'

'Exactly the way I want it, Harry. Thanks.'

The governor picked up his phone, made some calls. While he waited, McIntyre thought back to the telephone conversation he'd had with Bishop Wright after he'd discovered Sam Clancy wasn't on the list his secretary had provided. After an extended silence, the bishop had stuttered that he didn't know why Clancy hadn't appeared on the list, whereupon the detective asked to speak to his secretary. After an interminable delay, she'd come on the line, told him in a resentful tone that, since Clancy had had a recent bereavement she'd thought it best to leave him off. He'd dressed her down for interfering with police business and taken it no further. But it had left a sour taste.

A knock on the governor's door interrupted his musings. A prison officer marched in and a minute later McIntyre was following the same officer through a labyrinth of corridors, until they arrived at the allocated interview room.

'First man will be down in five minutes,' the officer told him, as he unlocked the door. 'I'll let him in and wait outside.'

McIntyre entered the room alone, sat at a desk which, like his chair, was bolted to the floor. The sickly green drabness of the walls were only interrupted by a thin barred window through which the detective glimpsed a patch of blue sky. It struck him, if you wanted to meditate, this could well be the ideal place because there was nothing here to please or distract the eye and thoughts would inevitably soon turn inward. No doubt many a prisoner had examined his past life here.

The first prisoner arrived. He proved to be a compulsive talker. McIntyre concluded his motivation for attending the priest's meetings was the promise of a piece of cake and the need for someone to listen to his incessant chatter. The man couldn't think why anyone would hold a grudge against poor Father Riley. Neither could the second prisoner, a compulsive arsonist with religious mania. In a stentorian rant, he claimed whoever had killed the good priest would burn in hellfire and that, if he got hold of the perpetrator, he'd save Satan the trouble and light a fire under him.

After the arsonist departed, McIntyre felt mentally drained, with nothing to show for his suffering. Then Ryan Todd slid into the room like an awkward schoolboy. His skin was so pale it seemed it had never seen the sun, his body so thin and bony he wouldn't have looked out of place in Belsen. This ghost of a man was a paedophile and child killer. McIntyre had to swallow a feeling of revulsion as he introduced himself and commenced the interview.

'You know Father Riley has been murdered,' he began, voice dry. 'I'm trying to discover whether anybody in here, or on the out, had a reason to want him dead.'

Todd gazed at the two-barred window as though afraid someone might be listening in. 'They say I killed a little girl,' he stated, his eyes everywhere except on the detective.

McIntyre was surprised to see tears running down his face but kept his expression blank.

'It wasn't me, you know,' Todd added conspiratorially, after a long pause. 'Not me at all. It was the devil got inside me, you see.'

McIntyre figured he wanted sympathy but he couldn't forget the little girl he'd killed, her devastated parents. How would he feel if it was his child? Did this man deserve any pity, any attempt at understanding? As though he'd read the detective's thoughts, Todd looked straight at him for the first time since he'd entered the room.

'The priest was the only one who showed me any sympathy . . . any understanding . . . it was as if he could see into my soul.'

Not really knowing the best way to respond, McIntyre's response was blunt. 'Part of his job, I suppose.'

'It was more than a job for him. It was a

157

vocation. He understood people like me . . . the sickness inside. Others thought the same.'

Todd had so far avoided answering McIntyre's question about whether anyone might want the priest dead. The detective wondered whether he might be seeing this interview as a break in a monotonous routine and wanted to extend it as long as possible. They were clever mites, some of these prisoners. With a sigh, he decided to get him right back on course.

'So Father Riley was an understanding person who couldn't possibly have an enemy in the world. Am I right? A simple yes or no would suffice, Ryan.'

'Yes!'

Todd lifted his eyes to the ceiling, as though he was transcending earthly bounds and contemplating the infinite.

'He said if I repented I'd be saved. Even a sinner like me.' The prisoner's eyes glistened. 'Do you believe that?'

Again, the little girl he'd killed flashed into McIntyre's mind. He managed to hide his distaste and gave a shrug.

'I'm not a priest. I don't know the mind of God, so let's move on, Ryan. Can you tell me anything about an ex-prisoner, name of Sam Clancy?'

When he'd asked the other prisoners the same question, he'd gathered Clancy was a quiet man who never bothered anyone and took his faith seriously. Going by that, he hadn't sounded like a priest killer.

'Sam Clancy was a thinker . . . a listener,' Todd said. 'He accepted the faith and became a believer like me.'

'One of the priest's successes,' McIntyre commented. 'I assume he and Father Riley must have become very close.'

'Yes . . . close! And other blessings came his way as a result of coming to the faith.'

'Blessings?'

'Love, Inspector, the greatest blessing of all. In this place of lost souls, he miraculously found love,' Todd sighed, wistfully. 'I keep hoping I will find such a blessing. I will know I am forgiven if I do.'

McIntyre disdained to comment on Todd's skewed logic. He wondered whether he was toying with him. Certainly he'd changed from the tearful, withdrawn man who'd entered the room. He had become quite garrulous. Schizophrenia came to mind.

'You mean he found love with a woman.'

'Yes! A good lady from Father Riley's church. Mary was her name, like the Holy Mother. She was a prison visitor. That's how they met. Happiness shone out of Sam

Clancy's eyes when she visited. We heard they married.'

McIntyre knew they had indeed married but didn't mention the suicides which would have contradicted Todd's rosy view that good things had happened to Clancy when he'd seen the light.

'I didn't like the nun,' Todd said, pulling a face. 'Bitch!'

'Nun?'

'Covered up . . . dressed in black. Don't like black. Devil's colour. Shouldn't come to this place looking like that, upsetting people. Eyes that could see right through you . . . made me shiver.'

Whoever she was, this nun had evidently got right under Todd's skin. McIntyre wondered how he managed to live with all his demons.

'Who was this nun?'

Todd shrugged. 'Don't know her name. She visited Clancy, came with Clancy's woman sometimes.'

McIntyre didn't consider the nun of much importance, except she might know something useful about Clancy.

'Nothing else?' he asked Todd, rather wearily.

Todd shook his head and the detective, pleased his work was done here at last, rose

160

from his chair to signal the end of the interview.

'Thanks for your help,' he said, his tone perfunctory. 'The officer will take you back now.'

'Pray for me,' Todd suddenly said, staring at the detective.

That took McIntyre by surprise. He muttered an affirmative while doubting whether he ever could pray for him.

Back in Harry Drew's office, McIntyre asked whether it was possible to have the name of the nun who'd visited Clancy. Harry told him there'd be a record in the visitor's book, that he'd phone him with the name later. Then the governor called for a prison officer to escort McIntyre out of the prison and they parted with a handshake.

The clean air and open space were welcome after the claustrophobia McIntyre had felt inside the prison walls. He always imagined the prison as a staging post on a journey to hell, those impregnable walls encapsulating all varieties of mental suffering. The idea made him depressed, even though he knew his own efforts had led to the incarceration of many of its past and present clientele. His visit had been a necessary chore and he hoped he wouldn't return any time soon.

20

The pristine white walls of the Incident Room were a welcome contrast to the malodorous smells that had pervaded the prison. McIntyre's colleagues were hard at it. Mac, absorbed with viewing the CCTV tapes, looked up briefly and acknowledged his boss, who noticed the strain in his eyes, no doubt the result of concentrating too long on the screen. Moira was at her desk, a sheet of paper held in each hand, head bobbing from one sheet to the other like a hen pecking at seed.

McIntyre made himself a coffee and sat down at a desk but was soon disturbed when Mac raised a beckoning hand. He carried his coffee over to his desk.

'There's a camera positioned at the exit from the car park,' the Scotsman said. 'I've got three women leaving around the time of the murder — not one of them a blonde though.' He pointed to the screen. 'But there is something here I want you to see.'

McIntyre leaned in and studied the frozen image on the screen. It showed a vehicle at the barrier, a figure wearing some kind of headdress in the driving seat. The lower part of the face was covered by what could have been a scarf, leaving only part of the facial features visible but not very clear.

'Thought it might be a Muslim,' Mac said, 'or someone who knows the camera is there using a disguise.'

'Did you get the number plate, Mac?'

'Plain as day. I'll run it through to the DVLA in a moment.'

McIntyre thought he saw something dangling from the driving mirror and pointed to the spot on the screen.

'Can you blow that up?'

Mac zoomed in and both men stared intensely at the object that appeared.

'It's a cross,' the Scotsman announced. 'Not likely she's a Muslim, then.'

Perplexed, McIntyre drew in a deep breath and frowned. Mac was right; she probably wasn't a Muslim. But it struck him that, dressed like that, she could very well be a nun. Would that be stretching coincidence too far when, only an hour ago, Ryan Todd had expressed his antipathy towards a certain nun he'd seen with Clancy's spouse?

'You having a revelation, boss?' Mac inquired, breaking the silence. 'Like the one that made you give up your season ticket at the football?'

McIntyre nodded. 'A glimmer, Mac, that's all. The faster you get me the name of the person the car's registered to, the faster I'll know if there's anything to it.'

Mac rose from his chair. 'Just wait here, boss. Won't take me long.'

McIntyre absent-mindedly sipped his coffee. If it was indeed a nun in that car, what was she doing on the campus late at night around the time the priest was killed? He put a break on his thoughts; it wouldn't do to get too far ahead of himself. How likely was it, really, that a nun would commit murder?

Mac soon returned and sat down again.

'The car's a red Micra registered to a Mary Clancy. Does that mean anything to you, boss?'

McIntyre felt something cold scuttling up and down his spine. He recalled Sam Clancy's wife had been called Mary. Could she be the owner of the car? Unless she'd risen from the grave, she couldn't have been driving that night. So who had?

Mac's voice broke his train of thought. 'There's another named driver.' He squinted at the piece of paper. 'Ann . . . Pebble. No, that's not right. Prebble. It says Prebble.'

McIntyre's memory stirred. Prebble! He was sure that was what Bishop Wright had called his secretary. Now it seemed the only person who could have driven the car legally was named Prebble. The secretary had acted strangely towards him and been obstructive right from the start. Undeniably separate strands of the investigation seemed to be converging in ways that it would be a stretch to call coincidence — but did it mean a solution to the murder was imminent or was it all a mere diversion away from the real murderer?

He stared at the screen, tried to make out the driver's features, to see if he could spot any resemblance to the secretary, but it was impossible. His gaze drifted to the bottom of the screen and what he spotted there shed a different light on matters.

Voice dry with disappointment, he told Mac, 'I had reason to suspect the driver might be involved but look at the time on the screen — two minutes past nine. The lecturer told us the priest was alive at 9 p.m. No way would two minutes have been long enough for the driver to do the deed and get to the car park.'

Mac looked sheepish; apologized in a chastened tone.

'Sorry about that, boss. Should have noticed, shouldn't I? The time shown will be correct. Campus security told me they're meticulous about such things.'

'Easy thing for you to miss when you're trawling through all that footage,' McIntyre told him. 'I didn't notice myself at first and, anyway, I think we've got something strange going on here.'

There was a moment's silence. Though the time might be wrong, McIntyre was curious about the driver of the car. Whoever it was, while not the perpetrator of the crime, could be connected to the murder in some way.

'Have a break from this,' he told Mac, gesturing at the screen. 'I'll do the follow-up on Ann Prebble.'

Back in his own office, he made his enquiries and what he discovered shed a very different light on the situation. Then he sat for a moment contemplating why the bishop hadn't mentioned his secretary was Sam Clancy's sister-in-law when they'd discussed her omission of his name from the list he'd requested. Now he was really suspicious about why Clancy's name was left off that list. Finally, he decided it was time to call the bishop.

He came up with a few reasons before he lifted the phone. The clergyman answered on the third ring and the detective came straight to the point.

'DI McIntyre here. Confirm for me your secretary's name is Ann Prebble, please,

166

Bishop, then tell me her connection to Mary Clancy.'

He heard a sharp intake of breath. It was followed by a silence which was too long and made him suspicious. He figured he must have hit a nerve if the bishop was struggling to answer.

'They're sisters,' the bishop said eventually, his tone much less ebullient than on their previous meeting and as wary as that of many a guilty man he'd put in the dock.

McIntyre was only a little surprised that Mary's sister was the named driver. He conjectured that it was possible Ann Prebble had left Sam Clancy off the list because he was her brother-in-law and recovering from a tragedy, not to mention he was also an ex con. But he needed to be sure.

'Had either sister any connection to a nun or nuns that you know of? Think carefully.'

Another hesitation, again far too long. This time McIntyre lost his patience.

'Is it a hard question, or is there some reason you don't want to answer it?'

He heard the bishop's painful sigh before the answer came with obvious reluctance.

'Ann Prebble used to be a nun, Inspector. She returned to the secular life several years ago. I gave her a job around that time. May I know why you ask?'

McIntyre smiled. He was making progress, even though he knew it might ultimately lead up a blind alley. Without answering the bishop, he continued with his own questions.

'Is she there now?'

This time the answer came almost too quickly. 'I'm afraid it's one of her days off.'

McIntyre could hear suppressed anger in the bishop's voice; the conversation was clearly not to his taste.

'I presume you have her home address.'

There was rustling of paper on the other end and then the bishop's voice came again with an address in Stockton, a town which almost adjoined Middlesbrough. The detective thanked him, mentioning he might be visiting him soon because he was now aware information was withheld on his first visit and he couldn't understand why. Before the bishop could reply, he put the phone down.

He stared at the ceiling for a moment, then leaned on his desk with his head in his hands, feeling dissatisfied. When all was said and done, if it was Ann Prebble driving the Micra, she hadn't had time to kill the priest and get to the car park by the time shown on the camera. The blonde, the caretaker and the lecturer remained the best suspects in spite of all he had discovered, so was he just wasting precious time?

A knock on the door brought him out of his reverie. Moira entered and placed two printouts on his desk.

'Father Brendan Riley and John Bright were contemporaries at Oxford, overlapping by a year,' she announced. 'But I'm not getting overexcited because John Bright studied English while Father Riley was history. They might never have met.'

McIntyre felt a surge of optimism in spite of Moira's reservations.

'Their paths must have crossed at some point.'

Moira shrugged. 'I spent a year living a few streets away from a cousin. Our paths never crossed. We can but hope, so I assume we'll be trying to find whether their lives intersected at Oxford.'

'There could be history between them,' McIntyre speculated. 'A longstanding grudge, for instance. Did anyone you spoke to in Teesside so much as hint they didn't get on?'

Moira shook her head. 'They only saw each other the night they taught in adjacent rooms, so nobody knew much about their relationship . . . if one existed.'

'Bright never mentioned their Oxford days to me.' McIntyre rubbed the back of his neck for a moment before he continued. 'Run with it, will you, Moira? Get on to those colleges, see if anyone remembers them. Better still, whether they were acquainted.'

Moira's face betrayed the fact she didn't relish the task.

'It's going to take time, boss, and an expensive phone bill. People move on.'

'Who better for the job than you, Moira, a woman of the world with enough Irish charm to melt the hearts of stiff-collared academics, circumventing all the red tape?'

She flashed her green eyes at him. 'And they say flattery is the last resort of scoundrels?'

McIntyre smiled. 'Maybe I've learned from our clientele, Moira. But you are perfect for this.'

'Even Inspector Morse had trouble with those Oxford dons,' she replied with a sigh. 'But I'll give it my best shot. You never know, I might even wangle a trip to Oxford.'

Their banter ended when the phone rang. It was Harry Drew from the prison with the news he had found the nun's name for him.

'My money's on Ann Prebble,' the detective interrupted before he could reveal it.

Harry laughed. 'You're fast on the ball for once, old son.'

'Yeah!' McIntyre said. 'Still got to run with it, though, haven't I? But thanks for your help anyway, Harry.'

21

Sam Clancy watched his sister-in-law attacking the kitchen floor so vigorously with a mop he thought she must be working off a mood. He wondered whether the reason was that she'd noticed he'd removed all traces of her sister and nephew or because he'd told her he intended to move out. All those dreadful weeks, she'd been there for him, cleaning, washing and ironing, while all he could do was sit and stare into space, his mind flooded with grief, struggling to cope. Not only that, she'd talked him through it, helped him to edge his way out of the dark pit he'd inhabited. Father Riley should have been the one doing that but the priest had made only one brief visit to him in his hour of greatest need. Thinking how the man who had changed his life and been so high in his estimation had let him down, he grew morose and put his head in his hands. His sister-in-law laid the mop down and faced him with a concerned expression.

'Come on, Sam,' she pleaded. 'Don't go back there. You've being doing so well.'

He brought his head up, stared into

imploring eyes that were so much like his wife's; he imagined just for a moment it really was her, that she'd come back to comfort him.

'Sorry, Ann. Got to keep up. It's just sometimes . . . '

'You still blame yourself, don't you?'

'How can I not?' he rasped.

Now her face was as pained as his, as though by osmosis his guilt had percolated through to her soul to show in her eyes and features.

'I'm her sister. Believe me, I'd know if it had anything to do with you. Something broke in her mind, Sam.'

'Even if that were so, we'll never know what it was, will we?' Clancy said. He thumped the table hard. 'That's what's killing me! Anything preying on her mind, I should have seen.'

She slumped down in a chair, groaning like an animal in pain. Her agony shocked him, sent shivers running up and down his spine. Her face was drawn tight, shrunken, as though all the troubles in her life had chosen that moment to reincarnate and, with that weight upon her, she'd metamorphosed into a much older woman.

'I hoped I wouldn't have to tell you!' she howled. 'But now I see I must or you'll go on torturing yourself.'

Shocked by that outburst and the transformation in her, Clancy put his hand on her shoulders and tried to comfort her.

'Tell me what, Ann? What's wrong?'

Like a condemned prisoner lifting fearful eyes to the gallows where the executioner awaits, she forced herself to look up at him. All the life seemed to have gone out of her eyes.

'It was my fault, not yours!' she moaned.

Clancy couldn't comprehend what she could possibly mean. She'd been close to her sister, never any hostility between them. Had the strain caught up with her after she'd been so strong for him? Was this a delayed reaction to the loss of her sister and nephew, manifesting itself now in a guilt trip of no real substance?

'I heard something that shattered my world,' she continued, her voice barely audible. 'Then I . . . I did the worst thing.'

Tears rolled down her cheeks. Mystified, lost in the fog of his own confusion, Clancy just stared at her.

'The worst thing?' he grunted after a prolonged silence. 'You said you did the worst thing.'

She clenched her fists, opened and closed them again and again, as though she was revving a motorcycle.

'Our departed priest,' she said, her voice sharp and bitter. 'He came to visit the bishop. It was my day off but I'd just popped in for something. They didn't know I was there. That's when I heard them. That's when everything changed.'

Her shoulders started to heave. Clancy leaned towards her, patted her head like a parent would a distressed child but she shied away from him like a cowed animal, shrank into herself again.

'You must tell me, Ann.'

She remained silent and he waited until eventually she took a deep breath, and without lifting her head began to speak in a trembling voice.

'Father Riley . . . he told the bishop that he'd . . . ' A piteous groan ascended from the pit of her stomach. Then, like a penitent in total despair and not believing salvation is possible such is the gravity of the sin, she continued, 'He said . . . he said . . . he'd abused poor little Tom.'

Clearly terrified, tears streaming down her cheeks, she risked a peek at Clancy. He didn't move a muscle, didn't even blink, sat there like a figure carved out of stone. Inside, though, his emotions were rampaging. He wanted to tell her she was mistaken, must have misheard but, judging from the depth of her pain, what she'd said had to be true. He had to fight for each word he uttered.

'What else did you hear?'

'The bishop told him to keep quiet about it,' she sobbed. 'I should have confronted them then and there but I ran out of the house in shock. How could I do that? How could I?'

He couldn't answer her and it was she who spoke strained words, whispered as though in the silence of a church.

'I went straight to Mary and told her. It was a stupid, stupid . . . stupid thing to do! She was distraught. We decided to go to the police . . . but she slipped away with Tom when I wasn't looking . . . '

Clancy stared at the table, imagining the state of his wife's mind. Tom was so precious to her and she was such a conscientious mother. His brain raced agonizingly over those occasions when the priest had been alone with his son. They'd both trusted him. Mary must have been in despair, felt she could never forgive herself, decided amidst her turmoil that she'd let their son down, that such an evil world was no place for Tom, that only God could take care of him properly. The priest had destroyed all she believed in and she couldn't go on. He was certain that's how it must have been.

Ann's voice interrupted his thoughts. 'I'm so sorry . . . so sorry. I can't forgive myself . . . ever.'

Clancy turned to her. Tears were streaming down her cheeks and he had no doubt she'd been in hell, torturing herself with her secret, trying to hide it from him, blaming herself, as he had been blaming himself. He knew about suffering; it was obvious she'd had a surfeit of it.

'You were in shock,' he mumbled. 'Blame that priest, not yourself.'

A car horn sounded on the street; the world outside intruding rudely into the melancholy silence of the room. It felt like sacrilege to him that people were going about their normal business while he was struggling to come to terms with what he'd just learned. Then a question leapt into his mind and he couldn't deny it a voice.

'One thing I don't understand . . . how could you go on working with the bishop afterwards? Do . . . nothing?'

'Revenge!' She spat out the word like a curse. 'You were hurt enough. I didn't want to hurt you more, decided to remove Riley from the face of the earth, then go after his conniving leader.' She hesitated, holding something back. Then it came out. 'I

176

searched the bishop's private files, found a letter. It made it clear Riley was suspected of abusing a child in his last diocese.'

Clancy winced. He was trying not to think about what Riley had done to his son. He'd already been on the brink of losing his sanity; knew if he went too far down that path again he might never recover. If Riley hadn't already been murdered, he was sure he would have done it himself. Then it struck him that Ann must have been equally driven. Had she murdered Riley?

'You're in trouble,' he said, forcing himself to concentrate. 'You'd better tell me every-thing.'

Weeping all the way through, she told him exactly what she'd done. When she'd finished, Clancy realized that grief and guilt had driven this mild-mannered, religious woman into actions he thought would be beyond her capabilities.

'I don't care what happens to me any more,' she groaned.

His sister-in-law's nerves were in shreds. She'd been there for him. Now she was the one needing help. Fighting his own sense of despair, he tried to assuage her feelings.

'We have to cope somehow, both of us. Mary wouldn't blame you and neither do I. And I know she wouldn't want to see either of us break, would she now?'

Those reassuring words, the fact he didn't hold her culpable, cheered her a little. They talked for a long time after that, mainly reminiscence about their loved ones, happy days they wouldn't forget. In spite of his own melancholia, when the conversation flagged, Clancy kept it flowing in order to distract her and that had the fortunate effect of helping him cope too.

22

McIntyre's visit to Ann Prebble's house proved fruitless, left him frustrated. Late that evening he arrived back at the Incident Room, sat down, stretched and stared out of the window at the Riverside Stadium, which was lit up like a magic circle in the night, lances of light shooting upward from its perimeter to disappear into the heavens. The match would be kicking off soon; he wouldn't have minded being there, losing himself in the game. He'd attended many times with his father until they'd put the prices up and he'd given up his season ticket, persuading his father to do likewise. Perhaps that hadn't been such a smart move because the games brought him and his father together, guaranteed he saw the old man fairly regularly. Now work or other things seemed to get in the way so they hardly saw each other.

Apart from himself, Moira was the only one left. He saw her reflection in the glass, like someone in a parallel universe, solitary and hunched over her computer, empty desks around her lending an eerie look to the room.

Salt of the earth was Moira. She deserved her husband, a really good bloke who didn't mind putting the kids to bed on his own.

When he turned away from the window and dreams of the stadium, she caught his eye and called out to him.

'Get yourself home, bonny lad. No good dreaming about the unattainable, which I warrant you're doing.'

He laughed. 'Yes, Mother. But take your own advice. Time you were off too. Those Oxford dons can ring you tomorrow . . . or you ring them. This time of night they'll probably already be in their cups.'

'I'll give it another half hour,' she said. 'The football traffic will have died down a bit by then.'

McIntyre was grateful for her dedication. Ann Prebble was now the cause of great suspicion but, if it was her in the car, the timing of her leaving the campus the night of the murder was all wrong. At best, she could be connected to the crime. John Bright remained a better candidate for it, but more ammunition was needed before he took him on again, something that would encase him in a straitjacket, no room to wriggle. Moira's research into his Oxford days might just provide that.

'No more than half an hour, then be off

with you,' he told her, when he was ready to leave.

He had one arm halfway into his coat sleeve when a phone rang. Moira beat him to it, told whoever was calling that McIntyre was only yards away. He gave her an inquiring look but she just shrugged as he took the phone from her.

'DI McIntyre here. Yes. Where did you say? Thanks. I'll be right there.'

'Not a spare ticket for the match, then. Not from that pained look,' Moira said as he put the phone back on its cradle.

'Could be . . . but only if I take it from a dead man,' he said, grinning ruefully. 'Dead body by the river, Moira. Definitely murder. Late-night jogger reported it.'

'Just what you need. You'll be lucky to get home by midnight.'

'Days merge in our job, don't they?' he said, waving as he headed for the door. 'Fact of life. No good dreaming about the unattainable.'

Ten minutes later he was standing on the river bank, his face lit by torches, headlights and intermittent blue flashes from the stationary patrol cars that had descended on the area, wishing he could soar above the river, fly in an instant to the men who had committed the atrocity that lay before his

181

eyes, make them pay for their degradation of what the word human was meant to symbolize. He didn't need superpowers, however, to know who was responsible for the body lying in the grass, nor to realize what it was meant to convey. This horrific slaying was a warning to every low-life in Middlesbrough that nobody could cross the king of their jungle with impunity. The tom-toms would probably already be sending that message across the town.

Billy Liddle's corpse was trussed up so tight in barbed wire it was a mass of lacerations. A mosaic of bruises patterned his chest where he'd been booted and beaten. His broken jaw hung open as though he had been about to start a question which he never managed to complete. McIntyre kept seeing visions of a dying fish, out of its element, struggling for that final breath. Billy was a tiddler in his world, too physically weak to put up a fight. Why couldn't they just have hooked him, warned him, then thrown him back? Even as he asked himself the question, he knew the answer was that Pike couldn't afford half measures or, sensing a weakness, the sharks would start to gather to pick him off.

'Just look what your botched operation has led to, DI McIntyre.'

The DI recognized the whining voice as belonging to the last person he wanted to confront at that moment. When he turned, Snaith was standing there in a heavy black coat, unbuttoned to expose a white shirt and dinner suit, his evening attire completed by a bow-tie. Even in torchlight, McIntyre could see he was incandescent and figured, if he knew his man as well as he thought he did, his irritation was as much due to leaving a warm hearth and a sumptuous meal as for any real concern for poor Billy Liddle. His accusation didn't do anything for McIntyre's own temper.

'From that remark, sir, I take it you know who did this. Could you be thinking of a certain Anthony Pike, by any chance, the man you told me to go cool on? If so, maybe you should have thought twice.'

'Be careful how you talk to me,' Snaith snapped back. 'You get nearer the edge every time we speak. Take it from me that your card is marked . . . in thick ink.'

McIntyre pointed to Billy's body. 'So was his, sir, because somebody had to have told Pike about him.'

The two policemen stood staring at each other, two rival stags sizing each other up, neither willing to give ground. Finally, with a sneering curl of his lip, Snaith lowered his antlers and spoke.

'Get away home. Somebody else can have this one. You need to concentrate on the priest. Don't suppose you've made any progress there, have you?'

'Working on it,' McIntyre said. 'But why deny me this? You know I'm the one most suited . . . know all the people to speak to. It makes no sense.'

Snaith swept a hand through his hair. 'I've told you to leave it. Conscientious is one thing, obsession another.' He pointed to the corpse. 'Tonight we've seen the result of your obsessive approach.'

McIntyre was furious, well aware if he answered back now he wouldn't be able to control himself. The floodgates would open and he'd say something that would put Snaith in a position where he'd have to do something. He'd already sailed close to the wind so, reluctantly, with nothing more potent than a loud sigh, he turned and walked away from the scene.

Driving away with a heavy heart, he had a moment of doubt, wondered whether Snaith might be right. He remembered his father saying that, where Pike was concerned, he was too involved and that might stop him seeing the woods for the trees. But, even if there was an element of truth there, at the

184

end of the day he knew he was too far down the line to ease up and he'd work behind Snaith's back to catch Pike. Billy Liddle's horrific fate had made it impossible to act otherwise. Meanwhile, he'd take advantage of Snaith dismissing him, get an earlier night than he'd expected and catch up on some much-needed sleep.

23

Bright and early next morning McIntyre knocked on Ann Prebble's door. Once again there was no answer but this time he hit lucky with one of her neighbours, who told him she could be at her brother-in-law's. Apparently she sometimes stayed there overnight because, according to the neighbour, the poor man, paralyzed with grief when he'd lost his wife and son, had been struggling to cope with the domestic chores. Unfortunately, the neighbour didn't have an address so McIntyre rang headquarters, who found Sam Clancy's address for him and he drove straight there.

A man with a lived-in face, melancholy eyes and a muscular body that hadn't been developed through weightlifting answered the door. His eyes measured McIntyre's length and the detective had the distinct impression he'd arrived at a bad time, was about as welcome as a bailiff with a final demand. When he held up his warrant card and introduced himself, the man looked distinctly unimpressed.

'Mr Clancy?'

'That was me last time I looked.'

Ignoring that ill-mannered, curt response, reflecting it probably originated from an ex con's aversion to the police, he asked politely whether he might come in and have a word. Though the man tried to hide it, McIntyre didn't miss the flicker of doubt in his eyes.

'Just a word, is it? I can just about spare a word, I suppose, but not too many. Words can be twisted, can't they?'

'Not by me,' McIntyre said, thinking the man seemed far too defensive and aware of how uncomfortable he looked as he stood back and beckoned him in with a jerk of his thumb.

When they entered the living room, the detective caught a whiff of perfume. He took a quick glance around, noted the dustpan lying on the hearth, a crumpled duster on the mantelpiece. Not offering his visitor a seat, Clancy stood in front of the gas fire, his arms folded, his expression long-suffering. McIntyre guessed he'd really meant it when he'd said he could just about spare a word.

'Actually,' he opened, 'it's your sister-in-law I've come to see, not you. I believe she's here cleaning for you.'

The question took Clancy by surprise. His eyes looked vacant, as though behind them his brain was groping desperately for an answer.

'Then you've wasted your time,' he said, eventually. 'She's been and gone.'

McIntyre smiled. 'The car at the door ... the Micra. I happen to know your sister-in-law has been using it.' He lowered his eyebrows, looked unwaveringly at Clancy. 'Maybe you're mistaken?'

In the clash of eyes, Clancy was the first to look away, an aura of sadness about him.

'Come on, Sam,' McIntyre said. 'Don't be obstructive. She's here, isn't she?'

Clancy didn't have time to answer before the door opened and Ann Prebble stepped into the room, lips quivering, face whiter than the paint on the door through which she'd entered. McIntyre remembered the controlled, self-possessed woman who'd irritated him so much on their first acquaintance. Her bearing was nothing like that on this occasion, more that of a woman on the edge of a nervous breakdown.

'It's OK, Sam,' she said in a voice straining for normality.

'Both of you should sit down,' McIntyre said. 'We need to talk.'

She drifted across the floor to the nearest chair like a sleepwalker. Clancy watched her all the way before slumping down into a chair as though he was drained of energy. McIntyre remained standing, one hand resting on the mantelpiece. A gloom pervaded the room. He cleared his throat, focused on the woman and got straight to it.

'You and I had a memorable meeting, Ann, so no need for introductions. The reason I'm here is for an explanation as to why CCTV footage shows you in your sister's car on the university campus, dressed as a nun, the night Father Riley was murdered.'

He was gambling because he couldn't be absolutely sure it was her driving. Would she deny it and, if so, how would he proceed from here?

She glanced at Sam Clancy, then spoke in a voice so quiet the detective could only just hear her.

'I went there to kill the priest.'

Clancy let out a long sigh and hung his head. His sister-in-law transferred her gaze to the detective.

'Start at the beginning,' McIntyre told her. 'I need to understand everything.'

She drew in a deep breath, told him how she'd overheard what the priest had done, how, blaming herself for the suicides and out of her mind with guilt, she'd decided to punish Riley herself.

'I drove onto the campus in disguise in the late afternoon,' she continued, 'parked there, walked into the town, returned at night, added a blonde wig and a hoodie to my disguise before I entered the building.'

'You were carrying a knife,' McIntyre said. 'Am I right?'

'Yes,' she agreed. 'I confronted that devil with a knife in one hand and an envelope containing Mary and Tom's ashes in the other.'

Clancy lifted his head. 'Ashes! You didn't mention that. Why their ashes, for God's sake?'

She raked her hands through her hair, shook her head.

'I must have been crazy. I wanted them to be part of it because I was doing it for them. You can see that, can't you?' Her eyes pleaded for understanding. 'I'm so sorry, Sam.'

McIntyre said, 'What happened in that classroom?'

'I couldn't do it. Something . . . maybe all my training as a nun, those years of believing a human life was precious, that every human life was worth something . . . prevented me. All I did was rail at him like a lunatic, throw the ashes at him and run out. Back in the car, I changed into my old nun's habit as an extra precaution.'

'And the knife?' he enquired. 'Did you take it with you?'

She shook her head. 'I dropped it on the floor before I fled.'

A picture of what he thought must have happened next flashed through the detective's mind but it was conjecture and he knew he'd have to be cautious, not lead.

'We haven't found the knife.'

Narrowing her eyes, she looked straight at him. 'You're thinking I did it, that I'm lying . . . but I'm not.'

'I don't think you did it,' McIntyre told her. 'CCTV showed the time you drove out of the car park. Riley had to have been killed between 9 and 9.15 p.m. You couldn't have done it and appeared at the exit in the time available to you.'

'So who do you think did it?' Clancy chipped in.

'I have a question that might help me find out,' McIntyre said. 'Did you stop on your way up to the classroom and look out of the window, Ann? Can you remember doing that?'

She didn't pause for thought. 'I definitely didn't stop.'

'So does that help you?' Clancy asked anxiously.

McIntyre wasn't sure. John Bright claimed he'd seen a blonde woman on the stair as he left, that she was looking out of the window.

Unless there was a second blonde, someone was lying and his money was on Bright.

'It might help,' he answered, turning back to Ann Prebble.

'Your brother-in-law knew nothing of your intentions?'

She shook her head. 'I only told Sam what I've told you a few hours ago . . . couldn't tell him at the time . . . he was so devastated I thought the truth would finish him.'

She began to cry while Sam Clancy sat there like a punch-drunk boxer, a faraway look in his eye. Finally, he gathered his wits and spoke up.

'It wasn't your fault, Ann. Something like that happens . . . it puts you on the road to madness. Believe me, I know.' He concentrated his gaze on the detective. 'What will happen to her now?'

McIntyre felt sorry for both of them, wanted to give them hope, believed there were grounds because what had happened to them was barely endurable and any right-thinking person would see that.

'Given how your state of mind must have been affected, I'm sure the law will view your actions very sympathetically. I'll do whatever I can for you, stress your emotional turmoil, how you've co-operated now.'

For the first time since he'd met her, she

192

looked at him with the trace of a smile. Though it didn't linger, he knew it was meant to convey her gratitude.

'You'll both need to come with me,' he told them.

As they were leaving the house, Sam Clancy patted McIntyre on the back.

'Thanks for going easy on her,' he said. 'Now that I think of it, I remember someone telling me about you. They weren't far short of the mark.'

24

McIntyre drew no pleasure from arresting Ann Prebble. The woman must have been overwhelmed with guilt, blaming herself for her sister and nephew's deaths, trying to shield her brother-in-law from the horrific truth, whilst another part of her was seething for justice and revenge. He doubted any normally sensitive person could have stood the strain. Fortunately for her, it looked as though she'd relented at the last moment, spared the priest.

Back at headquarters, he made sure she and Sam Clancy were treated well and led the formal interviews himself which, along with the paperwork involved, took up much of the rest of the day. The team's attention turned more to John Bright and Edward Wilson, though the possibility that one of Riley's criminal contacts, through his work at the prison, could have killed him, remained open. Moira informed him she'd received phone calls from Oxford but nothing of conse-quence so far.

The day after Ann's arrest, with no further progress made, McIntyre was ready to head home when his phone rang. The caller was distressed, voice so high-pitched it took a moment for him to realize it was Kate. When he'd calmed her down, she managed to explain herself. He told her he'd be at Done Roaming in ten minutes.

The door to Kate's flat was open and he found her in the living room perched on the edge of the sofa, cheeks wet with tears, arms clasped tight around her chest in a self-embrace. She'd already told him the reason for her distress and now he saw the corpse for himself. It was lying in front of the television, guts and blood spilling out of its stomach like lava from a volcano.

McIntyre felt sick. Two nights ago the sight of Billy Liddle's ruined body had affected him. Maybe it shouldn't be the case, but this seemed worse and he could feel tears forming.

'What kind of person could do that?' Kate sobbed.

McIntyre placed a hand on her shoulder. How should he answer her? The poor creature lying there had been less able to defend itself than Billy and he was remembering those nights when it had stretched out on his knee purring in contentment, trusting him to stroke its stomach. Had it trusted the stranger who'd ripped its stomach open? The

195

thought made him nauseous. Only an emotionally damaged person who didn't value life could have done such a thing. But what good would it do to tell Kate that? Her cat was dead. Nothing he said was going to bring it back.

'The door was open,' she groaned, with a shiver, as though the sound of her own voice frightened her. 'Maybe I left it open. Maybe that's how whoever it was got in . . . me to blame.'

'The lock wasn't broken and there's no sign of damage,' he said. 'Did anyone else have a key?'

She looked startled, as though he'd asked her to reveal a secret she'd been guarding with her life. Her reaction perplexed him because surely it was an innocuous enough question.

'You either left the door open or unlocked. The other possibility is that someone else has a key. What do you think, Kate?'

A void of silence opened up, broken only by the clock ticking in the background, like a finger drumming impatiently in a monotonous rhythm. McIntyre could tell Kate was in turmoil and when she answered him he could barely hear her voice.

'Nobody else has a key.'

He sensed she was lying. It was in her eyes,

the way she forced herself to hold his gaze, the way she tilted her chin defiantly, daring him to challenge her.

'We'll have to check nothing is missing,' he said, brusquely.

She nodded, without any real interest.

'Yes, I suppose.'

'Nobody has a grudge against you? Think hard!'

'No!'

Her uncommunicative mood was puzzling him. She was obviously distracted, preoccupied by a matter other than the one at hand. McIntyre was almost certain she hadn't left the door open or unlocked. In her line of work, she had to be conscientious about locking doors and cupboards and it was an ingrained habit. A silent impasse developed between them and was in danger of growing into a chasm until the phone rang and Kate grabbed it as though she was grateful for the interruption.

'It's for you,' she said, handing the phone to him.

McIntyre frowned. He hadn't told anybody he was coming here.

'McIntyre speaking!'

A muffled voice answered, 'How many lives has a cat got? More than a snitch, do you think?'

McIntyre closed his eyes, fought his fury. 'Who is this?'

'Never mind that. Stupid question. Just go to the bathroom and check out the cistern.' A chuckle came over the line. 'Have a good day now.'

The call ended and McIntyre held the phone at arm's length, staring at it with such grim focus it was as though he was attempting to drag the caller down the line by sheer force of will.

Kate noticed and stirred herself. 'What is it?'

Scowling, he grabbed her hand, pulled her off the sofa. She didn't protest as he led her into the bathroom, removed the top of the cistern, reached down and withdrew a bag of powder hanging by string. He dangled it in front of Kate like a fish.

She gasped. 'Cocaine!'

He picked up a pair of scissors he noticed on the window-sill, cut the bag open and used his finger to taste the powder. Kate watched, wide-eyed and perfectly still, as though held in thrall by his actions.

When he nodded affirmation, she took a step back, the implications hitting her hard so that her face turned as white as the sink where he'd laid the bag.

'You don't think I . . . '

She couldn't say it so he pre-empted her. 'No! I don't think!'

He explained the phone call then led her back to the living room, positive this was nothing to do with Kate but a warning from Pike, the gangster getting at him through her. It would be hard and he didn't relish the task but now he was going to have to tell her that her dead cat and the hidden drugs were a consequence of her association with him. How would she react to that?

He sat her down, explained it to her, each word a weight hauled reluctantly from his mouth. If there'd been a wall between them before, he was certain he was building it higher. Already, he had his suspicions she hated what he did for a living; this would surely be the final blow to their chances. When he'd finished talking, he waited for her to vent her anger on him but she surprised him by remaining in control.

'So Pike killed my poor cat and put the drugs in my bathroom as a warning to you?'

'Not him,' he answered warily, the fact she hadn't flown at him a consolation, though not sure he was out of the woods. 'Other people do his dirty work for him.'

Her next question synchronized with what he was wondering himself.

'Whoever it was, how did he get in the door

without breaking it?'

It was a straightforward question but he had an intuitive feeling there was something behind it she didn't want to share with him and, whatever it was, it was terrifying her. He was reluctant to draw it out, but before he had a chance to even try, a loud knocking on the door and a woman's voice shouting Kate's name interrupted.

He followed Kate into the hallway, stood close behind her when she opened the door. A grey-haired woman who looked frantic was standing there struggling to regain her breath. Since she was dressed in the same blue uniform which the staff in the home wore, he guessed she worked with Kate.

'What's wrong, Betty?' Kate asked.

Half turning away, Betty took a few steps backward and waved a hand, beckoning them to follow her. As they started towards the main building, she shouted over her shoulder, words tumbling out of her mouth so fast they were only just intelligible.

'Hurry! The residents have caught a burglar.'

McIntyre followed the two women into the main building, past the empty reception desk and into a long corridor. Muted voices came from one of the rooms ahead, then the familiar, unmistakable sound of a gunshot.

Heart pounding, he traced the sound to a half-open door and peered inside. An old woman with a hearing aid was sitting in a chair watching a television, the volume at full blast. Before she was even aware of his presence, he exited, shaking his head at the two waiting women.

Betty led them to another room where the door was open wide. He stepped in first and what met his eyes could have been mistaken for a scene from a comedy film if it hadn't been reality. At the far side of the room, an elderly man in a wheelchair was dabbing at his bleeding nose. Not far from his feet, three men, all well into their seventies, lay sprawled on top of a male figure attired in a grey tracksuit, his face partially hidden by a hood. A tired attempt to pull free was thwarted by the old boy lying across his stomach, rewarding him with a fist in his ribs. The same old boy was the first one in the room to notice McIntyre.

A gleam of triumph in his bloodshot eyes, he shouted enthusiastically, 'No need for panic! This one ain't going nowhere fast.'

The other two men glanced up at McIntyre. One of them, his cheeks puffed out, was holding onto the intruder's legs like a miser embracing a precious hoard. The other one, his face red and contorted with sheer determination, was using a pair of spindly arms to hold the burglar's shoulders against the floor. McIntyre had to reproach himself for a bizarre desire to shout 'Cut'.

'The coward smacked poor old Ted on the hooter,' Spindly Arms growled. 'Thought a bunch of old coffin dodgers would be easy meat. Selfish bastard didn't understand it's one for one and one for all in this place. We might live in Done Roaming but we're not done fighting.'

'I'm a policeman,' McIntyre said. 'But somehow I don't think you guys really need my help right now.'

The three old boys shook their heads in unison, like dogs shaking off tethers and revelling in newfound freedom. McIntyre turned to Kate, who hadn't spoken a word; he saw all her attention was focused on the infiltrator. She seemed stricken with fear and, as he made a move to embrace her, she sprang forward like a tigress, grabbed the grey hood and ripped it away from the burglar's head. Through bleary eyes, a young man looked up at Kate as though he had no idea where he was or what was going on. She reeled away from him, shaking her head. Then she covered her face with her hands and, before McIntyre could stop her, ran back into the corridor where her footsteps echoed like a burst from a machine gun. He exchanged a puzzled glance with Betty, who seemed as bemused as he was. He could only think she'd recognized the intruder and something about him had terrified her enough for her to run away like that. Though he wanted to, since he was the only policeman present, he had to stop himself from following her.

When at last the uniforms arrived, he hurried over to the flat, found Kate curled up in a chair, her head buried in a cushion she was holding against her chest like a comfort toy. He touched her shoulder gently and she stared at him with an expression he couldn't read.

'What is it, Kate?'

She dug her fingers into the arms of the chair, spoke to him in a voice that faltered.

'I . . . can't believe . . . he would do that.'

'Who is he, Kate? You obviously recognized him.'

She didn't answer, just stared into the corner of the room as though dismissing him.

'Not too much harm done, anyway,' he said, concerned and hoping that might assuage whatever was troubling her. 'That old man got a bloody nose and a scare but he'll be all right. Try not to get too wound up about it, Kate. The old codgers will enjoy being heroes for a day.'

In a forlorn voice, she mumbled something he didn't catch. Then she looked at him and, realizing he hadn't heard, spoke angrily.

'Didn't you hear? I said that was my brother.'

Her eyes grew piercing, precision drills exploring his face. He showed her no reaction, though he was shocked. For heaven's sake, he hadn't even been aware she had a brother. In the end, he nodded in a way he hoped would look to her like complicity.

'I'll help you get through this,' he muttered.

As he spoke, he glimpsed the cat's body still lying on the floor and a thought entered his mind to which he reluctantly gave voice.

'Did you give your brother a key?'

She knew the implication behind his question and flinched as though he'd struck her. In silence, he watched her face betraying the contradictory thoughts competing in her head like opposing tides.

'I gave my brother a key,' she said eventually, in a voice that sounded to him like a penitent's addressing her confessor.

McIntyre had his answer but he didn't want to press her with the next one. He preferred, if her brother was to be condemned, that she should initiate the act rather than him. Fortunately, she complied with that desire.

'How could he do that to my poor cat?' she cried out.

He wasn't sure whether the question was rhetorical or addressed to him, so again he kept quiet, hoping she would make the next leap without him. She didn't disappoint.

'Those drugs! He must have put them there.'

McIntyre shuffled his feet like a gauche schoolboy. It wasn't a pleasant experience watching Kate suffer from her suspicions. Judging by her brother's physical appearance, he was a drug addict and that would explain Kate's ambivalence towards him and his career, her attitude following that night in the restaurant.

'Your brother's a drug addict, isn't he?' he said gently.

She nodded assent and McIntyre thought he had a good idea what had happened. The way he saw it, Pike must have discovered she had a drug-addicted brother and incited him with the promise of drugs, or money, to act against his sister, though, driven by his craving, he'd probably made the decision to burgle the old people's home himself.

'The gangster you spoke about,' Kate said, bitterly, 'did he make my brother do this for him?'

'I'd say it's likely Pike offered him the drugs he craved in return for doing as he asked.'

'I gave him money and pleaded with him to come off them last time he came here and he told me he was trying.' A tear ran down her cheek. 'Was he taking me for a fool?'

McIntyre kept his counsel. She was gradually reaching the right conclusions herself, didn't need him to add his pennyworth. After a minute passed, she looked straight at him. When she spoke, her voice was stronger.

'I was angry with you that night in the restaurant. What you said about addicts made me feel helpless and ashamed. Guilt was the reason I didn't want to see you any more.'

'I understand,' he said. 'Right now you need to take some consolation from the fact something like this was always on the cards for your brother. As awful as it seems, it could have been worse and might yet turn out to be what saves him . . . in the long run.'

'Don't!' she exclaimed, holding up her hand. 'Don't patronize me, Don. The truth is Alan will go to prison. I know he deserves to but how can anything be worse than that for a young man?'

'It's better that than ending up killing someone, perhaps himself,' McIntyre came back at her. 'Besides, if he's willing, there are people in the prison to help him break his habit.' He sighed. 'It might look black, Kate, but there's hope and he'll need you to help him, that is if you can forgive him for what he did tonight.'

She wiped tears away with her handkerchief. 'You were right all along,' she said. 'I should have taken notice.'

'Alan's your brother, Kate. It was only natural you tried to protect him, wanted to believe he'd pull himself out of it.'

She glanced despairingly at her pet's body. 'How can I forget what's happened here?' She pointed to the corpse. 'Forget my brother did . . . that!'

McIntyre drew in a deep breath. 'The only way you'll come to terms with it is to tell yourself he was possessed by a demon which, in a way, he was. But right now, think of yourself — your job is involved here. When you're questioned, you have to say you didn't know your brother was using or you would never have allowed him access to your flat.'

Kate looked bemused, as though she'd been offered a gift but had reservations about accepting it.

'You mean I should lie?'

'It would be a white lie,' he said. 'However mistakenly, you tried to be loyal and help your brother. I don't think you deserve to suffer for that so I'll get rid of the drugs and nobody will be any wiser. I feel responsible anyway. If you hadn't been involved with me none of this would have happened.'

Kate looked at him in a way he'd never seen her look at him before.

'You'd take a risk like that for me?'

'You're an innocent party in my eyes,' he told her. 'If Alan happens to confess, they'll search and find nothing, think he was so high he was imagining it all.'

Kate pondered a moment then said anxiously, 'But will he mention the gangster?'

McIntyre shook his head. 'Pike works through other people. My guess is your brother probably had no direct contact with him and, even if he did, he'll probably be too frightened to mention his name.'

Suddenly, Kate leapt to her feet, and taking him by surprise slid her arms around his neck and buried her head in his shoulder like a vulnerable child seeking security.

'I suspected you were a hard-hearted policeman,' she mumbled. 'But I was wrong about you.' She drew back a little, looked him in the eye. 'I don't like you risking your job to help me, Don.'

McIntyre didn't need reminding he would be crossing a line. It wouldn't be easy but he figured the situation demanded it.

'I'm not naïve, Kate. I'm aware there are times when the law can't encompass all the angles. I want to avoid that happening to you. It's as simple as that.'

He eased her away from him, wanting to get it over and done with because that bag of cocaine was still in the bathroom and it was making him uncomfortable. The quicker he got rid of it the better he'd feel.

'I'll try to catch those uniformed boys before they take your brother away, see how the land lies. I'll take the cocaine with me now. Will you be OK?'

'I won't let you down,' she answered.

As he stepped into the night, the cocaine tucked in his coat, he remembered the shadowy figure he'd seen leaving through the same door a few nights before. That must have been her brother — not, as he'd imagined, a new boyfriend — and he chided himself for making assumptions.

Dumping the drugs in the boot of his car, he went back to reception where he found a policeman holding Kate's brother. Alan was calm enough, still looked out of it. Nearby, the old boys were being questioned and seemed to be basking in their moment of glory. He told the policeman Alan's identity and Kate's connection to the culprit, stressing he was sure from her reactions she had no idea what he'd been up to. They agreed that McIntyre would take her statement. After that, he said, since he wasn't needed, he'd be on his way.

Ten minutes later, at a remote spot on the banks of the River Tees, enshrouded in darkness, he removed the drugs from the car boot. He estimated the contents were worth a few thousand. Pike must have thought it worth the price tag to send him a warning. The innocuous-looking stuff he was holding was, he knew, a mere drop in the ocean compared to the amount that passed through the gangster's hands, but even that amount had the potential to bring misery, its tentacles spreading far beyond the users themselves. Kate and her brother were good examples. He launched the bag into the air with all his strength and heard it land in the water with a soft plopping sound. Then, glad to be rid of the stuff, he walked back to his car, reflecting on his action, telling himself it had been necessary and he could live with it.

25

Next morning McIntyre was at his desk, reflecting on the previous night's events when Moira knocked and entered his office. She looked as tired as he felt but there was a twinkle in her eye which he hoped meant she had good news for him.

'The halls of academe have responded at last,' she said. 'Phone call from a retired Oxford tutor. Would you believe he thought Middlesbrough was a few miles from the Roman Wall and that I was a Welsh woman? Imagine! When we sorted his geography and overcame linguistic difficulties, he was pretty informative. You'll like it.'

What she told McIntyre made him forget Kate's trouble and his tiredness. The information she'd received put John Bright right into the frame. A visit to the lecturer had suddenly become an urgent priority.

'Well done,' he told Moira, grinning. 'Those phone calls have paid off and at the same time improved cross-border relations in the United Kingdom.'

Moira gave him a sulky look. 'Too good for my own good, me. I was hoping for a trip down to Oxford, punt on the river, all expenses paid. A straw boater would have suited me too.'

'Dream on, girl!' McIntyre pulled on his jacket. 'Besides, what's better than a bag of prawns on Redcar beach with the wind blowing in wild off the North Sea? Might even treat you myself if this pays off.'

'That's all right for you indigenous types,' she scoffed. 'You've grown up with it. Anyway, talking of prawns, good luck with the great pretender, aka John not-so-Bright.'

McIntyre thanked her and started for the door, pretty sure that with the information she'd provided he'd be able to nail the lecturer to the ground. He was looking forward to it.

'Go get him, cowboy,' Moira shouted, making a gun barrel with her fingers.

26

Bright lived in Acklam, a pleasant area of the Boro. His home was a semi-detached house that, in spite of signs of decline, retained a certain grandeur which McIntyre figured would be its main appeal to a man who had a high opinion of himself. A brass plate on the wall near the door read 'John Bright BA', that ostentatious announcement seeming to fit the man's character to a tee. Given degrees were two a penny these days, it was extra pretentious to advertise his at the entrance to his domain.

A small woman answered McIntyre's knock. As she peered at the detective she exuded an aura of timidity and he noticed she was gripping the door with both hands as though she was guarding a secret place and no stranger would be permitted to cross the threshold unless he knew the password. He produced his warrant card in lieu of the password.

'Mrs Bright?'

She answered with an almost imperceptible nod.

'I'd like to speak to your husband, please. Is he in?'

She hesitated, fluttering her eyes as though temporarily blinded by a bright light. For a moment, he thought she was going to refuse him entry but then she opened the door wider and stepped back, which he interpreted as an invitation to enter. When he was in the passageway, she spoke in a quiet voice, her accent definitely not a local one.

'Follow me, please. He's in the conservatory.'

She led him to a spacious conservatory at the back of the house. It was built out into a garden whose privacy was guarded by tall trees. One side of the garden was lawned, while on the other side vegetables grew in neat rows. Oblivious to his visitor, John Bright was ensconced in an armchair, feet up on a stool, munching a piece of toast while he read a newspaper. He looked totally at ease but the detective didn't think that would last much longer.

'Inspector McIntyre's here to see you, John,' his wife announced, then slipped away as her husband turned his head in their direction.

Bright's shoulders stiffened when he recognized his visitor. His features twisted into an unpleasant glower and he let the paper fall to the floor in an untidy heap.

'Sorry to disturb you first day of your hols

and you looking so at ease with the world,' McIntyre said, not sorry at all.

The lecturer pointed to a chair and spoke through gritted teeth.

'Pray be seated, though I can't imagine what I can add to my previous statements that will elucidate the matter of Father Riley's unfortunate demise to any further degree.'

McIntyre sat in the chair and pointed to the vegetable plot. 'I see you like to keep your garden neat and tidy.' He placed a finger on the side of his head and rotated it like a screwdriver. 'I like everything neat and tidy in here, John, and the trouble with our priest's death is there are a few things not lining up in those neat rows.'

Bright forced a smile. 'I like your attempt at imagery, Inspector. Maybe you should try writing poetry.'

He reached down, picked up his cup and saucer and sipped his tea. If the action was meant to convey he was cool, it didn't work. The rattle when he placed the cup back on the saucer betrayed the fact he was nervous.

'I don't think I can help you tidy your imaginary garden,' he said.

'But you can help me kill off a few weeds, John, let a little light in. For instance, you said the priest was alive when you left your room at 9 p.m., and you noticed a blonde woman on the stair as you left. I've got that right, haven't I?'

'Precisely,' Bright replied, his eyes narrowing. 'The caretaker confirmed the time I left the building, didn't he?'

McIntyre gave a tight smile. 'It's not so much you. It's more to do with the blonde.'

Bright didn't say anything and assumed an air of studied insouciance, which didn't fool McIntyre. He figured he was probably aware of what was coming and was searching desperately for a way to counter it, so he kept quiet, letting him stew, and in the end Bright lost the battle of wills.

'No need for games, Inspector. You've caught the blonde and she's telling you a pack of lies.'

McIntyre nodded. 'Don't know about lies. She admits being in Riley's room but not to his murder. We know from CCTV she drove out of the car park at two minutes past nine.' He sighed. 'You see the problem, don't you? The nasty little weed trying to ruin my neat little garden is the timing, the fact that the blonde couldn't have done the dirty and made it from the building to the car park exit in two minutes. Don't think even Usain Bolt could do that.'

Bright stared at the detective, his face a picture of consternation. McIntyre watched him like a vulture ready to swoop at the first opportunity.

'Maybe it was a completely different blonde on the stair,' the lecturer offered. 'A student maybe.'

'I suppose it's possible,' McIntyre agreed, 'but, in truth, I'm starting to believe she was no more than a figment of your imagination . . . or . . . invented.'

McIntyre had played his high card. His words hung in the air and a long silence ensued while clouds drifted across the sun, creating moving shadows on the tiled floor as though the world was moving beneath their feet. Then, suddenly, there was another shadow, a pigeon swooping, flying straight at the glass, flapping its wings frenetically as it veered away at the last second.

'It wasn't my imagination and she wasn't made up,' Bright said, his voice wary, that cool cockiness definitely on the wane. He straightened his back. 'So what are you trying to imply?'

'That you're top of my pops,' McIntyre told him. 'That you've been lying and that makes you my chief suspect.'

Colouring up, the lecturer thumped the arm of his chair. 'This is outrageous. The woman existed, I tell you. Maybe it was a different blonde but she was there . . . on the stair . . . that's all there is to it.'

McIntyre tilted his head to one side. 'Oh, I'm well aware a blonde existed. She was in fact a brunette wearing a wig as a disguise but you never saw her standing on that stair.'

Bright saw a chance. His eyes gleamed. 'If she admits disguising herself, she must have killed him. Why are you accusing me?'

'She was in Riley's room about five minutes before 9 p.m. Intended to kill him, couldn't do it, dropped the knife and fled. By 9 p.m. she must have been well on the way to the car park. My opinion is you saw the blonde berate Riley and then leave. That was your opportunity and you used the knife which she had dropped.'

'You're mad!' Bright cried in fury. 'A thick plod who's fitting me up to hide his incompetence. I had no reason to want him dead.'

McIntyre smiled. He figured with a little more pressure the lecturer would probably crack. So far he'd been holding back his big guns. It was time to bring them to bear.

'An Oxford degree is a passport to success in life, so they tell me, a world away from being a thick plod.'

Bright snarled. 'How true . . . on both counts.'

'But they don't give that cherished

accolade to someone who cheats in his final exams, do they?' He paused, watching Bright's expression change from initial incomprehension to horror. 'It must be awful if that happens, like being . . . one degree under . . . for the rest of your days. A nearly but not quite.'

Bright recoiled as though struck by an invisible fist. His face turned a cadaverous grey colour.

'But then why am I telling you this?' McIntyre continued. 'You had to leave Oxford in disgrace for that very reason. That didn't suit you one bit, so you pretended you had a degree and were given teaching posts on the strength of a lie.'

Bright drew in a savage breath. He'd been exposed as a charlatan, yet he quickly pulled himself together and there was an air of defiance about him.

'I had the ability,' he said. 'As good a brain as any of my contemporaries.'

McIntyre raised an eyebrow. 'So good you had to cheat and lie, eh? You got away with it too, until the past came back to kick you in the teeth.'

Bright narrowed his eyes. 'What do you mean by that?'

'Riley attended the same church in Oxford as you did, so it must have been a big shock when you met him again after all these years. He remembered your fall from grace, made enquiries in Oxford and was ready to expose you. I figure he told you his intention and you killed him to save your bacon.'

Bright lowered his head and stared at the floor. The detective waited in silence until he looked up again and made one more tired attempt to obfuscate the issue.

'None of that's conclusive. Maybe I just thought I saw Riley in his classroom. Maybe I saw his body but didn't realize he was already dead. Maybe there was another blonde.'

McIntyre shook his head. 'Get real, John. That's an awful lot of maybes for any jury.'

As he finished speaking, a flurry of rain beat against the conservatory glass like a round of applause. Momentarily distracted, McIntyre looked out into the garden and watched a seagull swoop down to pluck a worm from the ground. The worm wriggled as the bird started to swallow it and he turned back to the lecturer, who seemed have aged ten years.

'You haven't got the knife,' Bright said, obdurate as ever, 'and no forensics either. You'd have said so if you had.'

McIntyre was only too aware that was the plain truth. He'd hoped the man would confess when he was exposed as an imposter, but it seemed he was going to hold out to the end. As for the knife, if they did find it, there was no guarantee his prints would be on it.

'Guess I'll just have to — '

Before he could finish his sentence he was interrupted by a loud bang. Both men turned towards the door to see Mrs Bright standing there, arms rigid as pokers, fists bunched. She no longer looked the diminutive, timid creature who'd let the detective in but more like a ferocious, wild animal ready to go on the attack. McIntyre figured she'd heard him accuse her husband and braced himself for an onslaught.

27

Sam Clancy was alone in the house, feeling restless. Now that he knew the reason why his wife had killed herself and their precious child, the priest kept looming in his mind like an ogre in a child's nightmare. It seemed a paradox beyond belief that the man who'd helped him change his life and given him hope had destroyed his future. Shouldn't he have seen through the priest, known him for what he was? Hadn't there been a moment during their long conversations when he'd revealed himself? Had all those fine words that had come to mean something to him and led to his conversion been no more than well-practised, meaningless cant on the lips of a hypocrite? His wife's faith had been so strong it made him weep to think how a man of the Church had betrayed her trust. His own faith had been battered, but there was a small part of him that was reluctant to let it go because it had made him a better man than he'd been before and deep down he knew it.

A better man! Those words resounded in his head. The jobs he'd done for Pike recently had skirted on the borders of legality and his next one involved a drugs deal. His intention had been to submerge himself in the old life but it was dawning on him that it wasn't for him any more and his conscience was bothering him. For the present, though, he'd hang in, figure a way to hit back at Pike.

A knock on the door broke his reverie. When he answered it, he found Joan Burton on the step, breathing hard and clutching a sports bag to her bosom as though it were a newborn infant. From the way she kept glancing furtively up and down the street, it was obvious she was in an agitated state.

'Can I come in for just a second?' she said. 'It's important.'

Perplexed, he stood aside to allow her to enter, then shut the door.

'Go into the living room,' he told her. 'I'll fetch a pot of tea I've got brewing.'

She placed the sports bag between her feet. 'Better to say what I've got to say here.'

He noticed she was wearing gloves though it wasn't particularly cold.

'Just go in and sit down, for pity's sake.'

'I can't, Sam, not until I tell you what I've done. You might not want me in your house after that.'

'I'm sure it can't be that bad, lass. Come away in.'

He reached for the sports bag but she beat him to it, swept it up like a petulant child unwilling to share a toy. Shaking his head angrily, he entered the living room, giving her no choice but to follow. She sat down as tentatively as a shy girl at her first party.

Clancy settled into his own chair. She was taking a risk coming to his house, he knew, and yet he sensed there was more to her current mood than fear that Pike might find out.

Swallowing hard, her voice croaking, she started to explain. 'I've decided to get away from him, to get away from Middlesbrough . . . a new start where I won't be found.'

'Best thing you could do. But why so glum? You should be happy.'

She focused on his face. 'I'm scared, Sam.' After a moment's pause, she added, 'It would help if you would come with me . . . a new start for both of us.'

The invitation took him by surprise. Another time and place he might have been tempted but right now Mary was still in his thoughts and he had Pike to pay back.

'I can't, Joan. I have unfinished business here. You know that.'

A disappointed look flitted across her face. She smiled enigmatically.

'Thought so . . . but it was worth a try.' She

took a deep breath and patted the bag on her lap. 'I let you down all those years ago, Sam, feel I owe you, so I've brought you this. It might help you and it certainly guarantees I won't ever be tempted to come back to Middlesbrough.'

She put the bag on the floor, unzipped it, reached inside. Clancy watched in amazement as she extracted one bag of white powder, then another. Before she could remove a third, he leaned forward and gripped her arm.

'What have you done?' he cried, a prickling sensation in his spine.

Their eyes locked. 'There's ten bags of coke here. Pike kept them under the floorboards in a flat he used as a bolt-hole. Nobody except me knew about the place. One day I was cleaning it for him and saw him hide this stuff.' She shook her head. 'Shows what a nonentity I was to him, doesn't it?'

Clancy was struck dumb. For sure, she would be the gangster's chief suspect. It was more than serious and probably too late to rectify. Pike would pull out all the stops to find her and the fact her actions coincided with his own reappearance on the scene wouldn't go unnoticed.

'I did it for you,' she repeated. 'I saw him

touching those bags so his prints will be on them. You can take it to the police and you'll have your revenge.'

Clancy still didn't know what to say. She'd risked so much for him — but naïvely. A maelstrom swirled his brain and he tried to order his thoughts.

'If I take this to the police,' he said, feeling his way, 'given fingerprints, they might be able to do him for possession, possibly stretch that to supply. But it won't be clear cut. I can foresee problems.'

Her eyes widened. 'I haven't touched the stuff. Neither have you. Surely . . . '

He grinned sardonically. 'I was in prison for drugs. Pike's side might say I set him up, that he handled the bags in all innocence. Those lawyers find loopholes, argue black is white.'

'I never thought . . . '

'That apart,' Clancy continued, 'even if he's convicted, he might only get seven years, much less with time off. When he got out you'd be looking over your shoulder and so would I.'

As she realized she hadn't thought it through, Joan's shoulders sagged.

'He deserves life,' she mumbled. 'The things he's done, never mind what he did to you.'

A plan started to form in Clancy's head. If he could pull it off, it might just retrieve the situation, turn Joan's actions to their advantage. However, it would depend on others playing a part as much as his own initiative.

'Did he ever rat on anyone else the way he did on me, Joan?'

'Of course he did. He boasted to me he had coppers in his pocket. I can name one or two rivals he set up. Must have thought he could tell me that because I was too stupid and too dependent.' She let out a sigh. 'He was right, I suppose.'

Clancy glanced at a picture hanging on the wall, one he particularly liked, a sheepdog running free on a hillside, wind pinning its ears back and ruffling its coat. He'd bought it soon after his release, attracted by the sense of freedom it conveyed.

'Well, you've proved him wrong now, Joan. But are you prepared to take another step, one that will finish him?'

She shrugged. 'All I know is the further from that swine I am the better I'll feel.'

Clancy hesitated. Joan had been an important part of his past. He was fond of her and he didn't want to place her in any kind of danger. On the other hand, if his plan succeeded, it would mean she could live her life without having to look over her shoulder. In the end, he decided he'd put it to her and she'd have to decide for herself.

'I think I can send Pike away for a long time,' he told her. 'You can make doubly sure of that if you testify he set me up using bent coppers and name the others he did it to. He'll be an old man before he gets out, if he survives when people know he's a grass.'

Joan took a minute to consider before she answered tentatively.

'But surely he'll find a way to shut me up before I can testify.'

'The police will protect you and his own kind will hate him. Nobody will do anything for him. He'll be finished, living in fear for his own life inside.'

Racked with indecision, she fell silent. Clancy could see she was tempted but afraid. He decided she needed more time.

'I'll make us some fresh tea,' he said. 'Give you time to have a think. Whatever you decide, it's OK with me.'

When he returned she was still looking pensive. He thought it likely she wouldn't want to testify. Who could blame her, really? Then she surprised him.

'I'll do it, Sam. But I'd like to be sent to one of those places they get you off the drugs while Pike waits for trial.' She gave the sports bag a meaningful thump. 'That stuff . . . it's been my ruin. Perhaps this is my chance . . . '

She didn't need to finish and Clancy smiled at her. 'Best thing you could do for yourself.' He hesitated. 'You do know I wouldn't ask if I didn't think it the safest thing for you . . . in the long run.'

She stared into the mug of tea he'd handed her. 'I trust you, Sam. I just hope your plan works.'

He rose from his chair. 'How long do you reckon before he notices those drugs are missing?'

'Could be a long time. He hardly uses that flat. It's really for emergencies.'

It was what he'd hoped she'd say. With luck, Pike wouldn't notice Joan was missing for a few days and he'd have time to make his arrangements.

'I'll have to hide you for now, just in case he comes looking. The loft would be safest. There's a camp bed up there.'

She managed a smile. 'You certainly know how to treat a girl.'

He told her the other part of his plan then made her an omelette and sorted out the loft for her while she ate. After she'd settled for the night, he hid the sports bag and made the phone call which would set things rolling.

28

John Bright's wife sped across the conservatory like a missile locked onto its target. No longer was there any sign of the subservient woman who'd led McIntyre into her husband's presence like a humble retainer bringing a visitor to her lord and master.

The policeman didn't have time to move a muscle and watched open mouthed as, with a swipe of her hand, she knocked the tea and toast off the table. She followed that up with a venomous slap which left an imprint on her husband's cheek. Then she pushed her face so close to his he couldn't bear its proximity and reeled back.

'Tell him,' she snarled, as Bright cowered behind raised hands, 'or I will.'

Bright stared at her as though he couldn't believe this vixen haranguing him was his wife. Withering visibly, he buried his head in his hands, but there was no escaping her ire as she recommenced her attack, flailing at his head with bunched fists until McIntyre pulled her off. Drawing in deep breaths, she relented, though the fire of battle still burnt fiercely in her eyes. McIntyre stood between her and her husband until he thought she'd regained control.

'Talk to me, Mrs Bright,' he said. 'Tell me what's brought you to this.'

She looked up at the detective, then back at her husband, who was staring into the distance as though wishing he was anywhere but in that place.

'I knew he was a charlatan,' his wife proclaimed, jabbing a finger in her husband's direction. 'All these years I knew, but I lived with it because I thought no one else would want me, that, for all his faults, he loved me a little.' She grimaced. 'What a fool I was. If I'd only known what he was capable of, the depths of his duplicity.'

McIntyre glanced at Bright, who seemed to have retreated into his own world and didn't appear to be listening.

'Can you elaborate on that statement, Mrs Bright?' he asked.

As though it was a relief to unleash emotions she'd battened down for too long, she didn't hesitate, told him how, as an impressionable seventeen-year-old working in administration at Oxford University, she'd been swept off her feet by Bright, who'd told her he wanted to marry her when his studies had finished. When he was sent down for cheating in his final exams, her life

231

came to a crossroads.

'Anyone else would have had second thoughts about him,' she said, with self-loathing. 'This little fool convinced herself to be loyal.'

McIntyre glanced at the lecturer. The vein in his temple was pulsating so violently it seemed ready to burst through the skin.

'He got round you with fancy talk, did he?'

Her eyes darted to her husband. 'He told me he cheated because our relationship had distracted him from his studies, that he'd done it for both of us, our future together.' She gave a shiver, her youthful credulity clearly disturbing to contemplate now. 'He pleaded with me to help him.'

'Let me guess what he asked you to do,' McIntyre said when she hesitated. 'Your work gave you access to student records. He wanted you to falsify his to make it appear he'd graduated.'

She covered her eyes for a moment before looking guiltily at the detective and nodding silent affirmation.

'He kept at me until I gave in and did his bidding. We soon married and he built his career on a lie. Anyone who bothered to check would find his qualifications in order . . . thanks to me.' She gave a little shiver. 'In this cold, northern outpost the past caught up with us.'

'In the form of a priest?'

She frowned. 'You seem to know a lot, Inspector. But what you really need to know is that beneath all the fancy words, the pretentious veneer, the man I married is not just a fraud but a cold-blooded killer.'

Bright at last turned towards his wife, his eyes pleading for her to stop.

'You're telling me he murdered Father Riley?' McIntyre said.

'Yes!' Her voice was as shrill as the north wind. 'My husband, who thinks he's so clever, is a common murderer.' With a disdainful curl of her lips, she pointed a finger at Bright. 'He believed I was still that stupid young girl and told me he had to kill the priest to protect our future. Imagine! That same, tired excuse. He was so confident he could twist me round his little finger he even showed me the knife before he buried it.' She jerked her head towards the garden. 'Out there, at the foot of the largest tree. Fancy being stupid enough to bury it in your own garden.'

Bright groaned. His wife had condemned him.

'Why didn't you tell us straightaway?' McIntyre asked. 'Why wait until now?'

She'd exulted in exposing her husband.

Now her shoulders sagged in defeat.

'I was worried about those papers I forged back in Oxford and, despite coming to realize he was flawed, I tried hard to be a loyal wife all these years.' She sighed. 'The priest's murder woke me up. Your coming here was the final push I needed to break out of my dream world.'

Bright hadn't moved. He looked broken, not one jot of that pompous affectation left in him.

'Want to add anything, Mr Bright?' McIntyre asked.

The lecturer seemed not to hear. He stared vaguely through the glass at his vegetable plot as though his only concern was that the rain would flood it. McIntyre turned his attention back to the wife.

'I'm going to arrest your husband,' he told her. 'I'll ring for transport, which will take you both to police headquarters. A team will come and search for the knife.' He paused there. 'You'll be arrested as well.'

She looked around the conservatory. 'I'm just glad it's over. This is a nice house but it's who you share a home with that counts. I'll pay my dues, whatever they may be. Afterwards, well, I'll know what it's like to be truly free. Being on my own doesn't scare me the way it did that naïve seventeen-year-old.'

234

McIntyre felt sorry for the way a mistake in her teens had ruined her life, bound her to her fool of a husband. But he was circumspect about her motives too because, at any time in the intervening years, she could have confessed and ended her torment. Perhaps she'd revealed only a corrupted version of the truth, the reality being she'd enjoyed the money and status being married to Bright gave her until the crisis point came when she'd acted in her own best interests. Whatever, he was glad the mouse had decided to roar. As for her husband's future, without a personality transplant he'd struggle to survive in prison. His fellow inmates wouldn't stand for his intellectual posing and would cut him to ribbons, maybe literally.

29

Two days after Joan Burton had turned up on his doorstep, Sam Clancy, following instructions Pike had given him, picked up one of the gangster's cars from a backstreet garage and headed through the mid-morning traffic, his destination the iconic Transporter Bridge which spanned the River Tees between Middlesbrough and Port Clarence. The bridge was a feat of engineering, the second largest of its kind in the world. Its travelling car, or gondola, was suspended by steel cables and ran on a wheel and rail system, crossing the river in 90 seconds, carrying a maximum of six cars. For hardier souls, there was a footbridge 160 feet up from the water. Clancy wished it had never been built. His wife and son's lives had ended falling from its dizzying heights into the cold waters of the Tees, so for him it was more metal monster than icon. He hoped it was no ill omen that the business he was involved in today was to be conducted within a stone's throw of the bridge.

Leaving the busy town, he drove the quieter approach roads, then down Ferry

Road towards the embarkation point. As the bridge towered ahead of him, he felt his stomach tighten and it took all his strength of will to stop himself imagining those last moments as his wife and son looked down at the long drop from which there would be no return and which had taken them away from him forever.

Only two cars were in the queue for the ferry and the gondola was on the far side of the river, crawling towards them like a gigantic spider suspended on gossamer strands. While he waited in the queue, Clancy scanned the area, looking for Pike, hoping there'd be no last-minute change of plan. The gangster said he'd arrive at the last minute but he was certainly cutting it fine.

Soon the gondola arrived at the Middlesbrough side, creaking and groaning, and locked on to the landing area. At first, Clancy didn't recognize the man in the flat cap, muffler and voluminous coat who opened the passenger door and lowered himself into the adjacent seat. When he saw that it was Pike, he breathed a sigh of relief.

'You look nervous old son,' Pike grunted. 'Suppose it's been a long time since you've crossed the water . . . or the line.'

Clancy raised his eyes to the bridge.

'There's bad memories here for me,' he muttered. 'Bad karma.'

'I forgot about that,' Pike said. 'Forgot your old woman took the plunge.'

Mary's name on the gangster's lips, never mind his callous words, was like sacrilege but Clancy managed to keep his temper, look straight ahead and hide his disgust.

'Took the boy with her,' Pike continued, not letting it go. 'Shame, that, but life goes on . . . onwards and upwards, eh! No good dragging the past along with us.'

Clancy's knuckles turned into bloodless peaks as he gripped the steering wheel. How had Joan tolerated this excuse for a human being for so long? he wondered.

A workman stepped forward to guide them on to the ferry. Clancy drove on and parked close to the vehicle in front. When all the vehicles were settled, the barrier came down and with a cacophonous grinding the gondola lifted clear of the dock and swung out over the river. As the ferry moved off, Clancy had a feeling of helplessness, as though he was a creature being carried to his fate in a predator's talons and there was nothing he could do now to change what was predestined.

'Why isn't someone doing this for you?' he asked Pike, to distract himself from worrying thoughts. 'Thought you didn't take any risks these days.'

Pike laughed. 'The fella I'm meeting is one paranoid Geordie with a contract on his head. He won't go into the town and he'll only deal with the main man. We go back a long way so he trusts me as much as he trusts anyone.'

'But why use the ferry?'

'There's only a few cars can cross at a time and the trip only takes 90 seconds. That means it's nigh on impossible for the bizzies to set up a trap. The guy has men watching the roads his side. Anything suspicious he'll know and call it off. I've got guys watching on the Boro side.'

'Suppose the Geordie tries it on?'

Clancy was aware of Pike's piggy eyes scrutinizing him.

'He won't. I trust him like I trust you, Sam.'

Clancy knew that was a downright lie. He could feel himself starting to sweat because he didn't like the way Pike had looked at him and the fact the gangster said he had no back-up. Playing a lone role wasn't his style. But the gondola was at the landing stage now so he had to put those fears aside.

'Keep well away from the Geordie's car and keep an eye open,' Pike said. 'I'll make the exchange inside his car while you join the queue, if there is one, for the return trip. I'll bring the goody bag and put it in the boot. Main thing is we get back on the ferry quick.' He patted Clancy's shoulder paternally. 'And don't worry, I've done this twice before . . . no problems.'

Clancy nodded. 'You're not carrying any cash?'

Pike grinned, patted his coat. 'You didn't notice I put on a few pounds, then.'

Before he could reply, the gondola locked on and the barrier lifted. A supervisor waved the cars off and when they were back on solid ground Pike pointed to a black Lexus parked near the landing area. Clancy parked ten yards behind it and the gangster got out and strode towards it. Once Pike had disappeared into the Lexus, Clancy waited until the ferry had moved off again then parked behind a Renault that had begun a queue for the next embarkation.

While he waited, he checked out the surroundings. There was nobody about except at a nearby hut, which sold tea and sandwiches, where a man was leaning on the counter supping from a mug, his free arm wrapped around a well-built woman who looked heavily pregnant and bored. As Clancy watched, the same man threw away the dregs of his tea and with great solicitude helped the woman into a Metro and drove up behind Clancy.

Moments later Pike emerged from the Lexus carrying a bag under his arm. The Lexus sped off straightaway and Clancy figured the deal had been done without any hiccups. Through the driver's mirror he watched Pike approach the Mazda, open the boot and deposit the bag inside. When that was done he came round to the passenger side and climbed in.

'Easy peasy,' he said, as he settled back in the seat. 'Told you, didn't I?'

'Be glad when we're back on the Boro side,' Clancy answered.

The ferry moved off and they were soon suspended over the river on the way back. Clancy was nervous, fighting off the tragic memories, that feeling of claustrophobia with him again. Pike noticed he was out of sorts.

'Don't look so uptight,' Pike said, grinning. 'No need for it, mate. Nobody but me and you knew this was going down today and we're almost home and dry.'

30

McIntyre shifted in the Renault's seat, pulled the baseball cap lower and fought the temptation to glance in the mirror at the occupants of the Mazda. He told himself to be patient. Only a few more seconds and he'd be off the ferry and bringing an end to Pike's reign. Yet he couldn't help remembering the sound of Pike's ringing laughter when, the last time he thought he'd had him, he'd walked away like a strutting peacock. That laughter still tormented him, even more so after Billy Liddle's tragic fate.

When the barrier lifted at last, he put the Renault in first gear and edged his way onto the terminal, driving like an over-cautious pensioner. Just once, he risked a glance in the wing mirror to reassure himself the other cars were directly behind.

Timing and distances were all important; had to be just right. Choosing his moment, he jammed his foot on the brake, then reversed. The crunch and scraping sound as he hit the Mazda's front end was music to his ears. Further back, the same sound repeated as the Metro drove into the back of Pike's car. The manoeuvre had worked perfectly. The gangster's car was trapped between the unmarked police vehicles, leaving Pike no way out.

He reached the Mazda's passenger door at the same time as his male colleague from the Metro, while the plain clothes policewoman cast the cushion that had acted as a bump aside and went for the driver's door. Pike looked up into his face with a pout that would have done justice to a trumpet player. It gave McIntyre the confidence to believe that this time he had him where he wanted him. But the pout disappeared quickly and was replaced by a jovial grin.

'Baseball cap suits you,' he said, laughing in McIntyre's face. 'So does premature senility.'

A doubt started in McIntyre's mind then. Pike had always been a cool customer in his dealings with the police, quick with the stupid wisecracks. He was running true to form and that niggled away at his innards like indigestion. Yet he was certain nobody could have warned the gangster because he'd set the trap up on his own initiative, and used only those he could trust to help him.

'Get out of the car!' he ordered, trying to dismiss any doubts he had.

With a big smile, mumbling something about police harassment and wasting the taxpayer's money, Pike complied. Clancy was already standing on the other side of the car next to the policewoman and exchanged a furtive glance with McIntyre across the top of the vehicle.

'Now don't you go worrying your little cotton socks off, Sam,' Pike said. 'Your old mate is as hard to hook as the slippery fish which bears his name. Has a bite too when he's crossed.'

The sinister undertones of those words worried McIntyre. The gangster still didn't seem as rattled as a man caught with the proceeds of a drug deal ought to be, either that or he was putting up a good show and hiding his feelings. The detective gritted his teeth, hoping it was all bravado.

'You've been stopped because I suspect you've been buying drugs,' he said, then turned to his colleagues. 'Keep an eye on these two while I search.'

A discreetly positioned colleague had videoed the gangster's activities on the other side of the river so if he found drugs McIntyre knew he'd be able to hang Pike out to dry. He approached the damaged boot nervously, aware this was the moment of truth and remembering with a certain trepidation he'd set this up without permission. Pausing to wipe away sweat gathering on his brow, he drew in a deep breath, pressed the catch, lifted the boot and was relieved to see the bag sitting there. He picked it up, carried it to the front of the car and dumped it ostentatiously on top of the bonnet close to where Pike was standing. Pike just grinned broadly.

'What have we got in here?' McIntyre exclaimed. 'Dirty laundry, perchance?'

Pike didn't seem to be in the least concerned. 'Take a look for yourself, Inspector Clouseau. But I warn you, you'll find it hard to stomach. In fact you'll hardly be able to bear it.'

Pike chortled to himself as though he'd cracked another great joke; hardly the behaviour of a man who could be facing a prison sentence. McIntyre was worried now and with a hollow feeling in the pit of his stomach, he tugged at the zip and opened the bag.

His fingers felt something soft and furry which at first he thought could be a dead animal, a gruesome joke which would be typical of Pike's warped mind. A bundle of brown fur fell onto the bonnet when he tipped the bag and for a moment he thought it really was a small body with a missing arm and leg and two coal black eyes staring up at him.

'Meet Rupert the Bear,' the gangster said,

smiling triumphantly. 'Cute, isn't he?'

McIntyre's heart was in his boots. He flipped the bear onto its belly and in a fleeting moment of optimism pulled at the zip on its back and felt inside. All he found there was rags.

Mock serious, Pike commented, 'Nothing is ever exactly as it seems, is it now? But I suppose you must be getting used to that. False appearances, I mean.'

McIntyre stole a glance at Clancy. He looked as surprised and disappointed as he was himself.

'Talking about false appearances,' Pike said, an edge to his voice, 'I'm beginning to wonder about my old pal Sam over there. Is he really what he seems?'

McIntyre was trying to figure how Pike could have known he was going to be stopped and searched. From the gangster's last comment, he suspected Sam Clancy's information had been genuine but Pike had rumbled him, played along to humiliate the police. The only thing he felt certain about was that there was probably more chance of him making Chief Constable than of finding any drugs in the Mazda. He'd gambled big time on Clancy's information, played the maverick, dragged his young colleagues into his scheme and all for nothing because, no matter how much it stuck in his craw, he'd have to let Pike go. When Snaith heard, there'd be hell to pay and he'd have to shield his colleagues. Those worrying thoughts chased around in his head as he tried to think of something to say to Pike that wouldn't sound like abject surrender and fuel his ego further.

'A word, Inspector, please.'

It was Clancy speaking. He beckoned to McIntyre, who walked around the car to speak to him out of Pike's earshot.

'He knew but I'm baffled how,' Clancy said in a whisper. 'But don't worry, we can still get him.'

The detective gave him a doubtful look. 'Maybe when Joan Burton testifies, yes. But not now, not today.'

'Take another look in the boot, Inspector, where the spare wheel should be.'

McIntyre frowned. Was this another wind-up?

'You heard Pike,' Clancy said, seeing his hesitation. 'He has his doubts about me, hasn't he? I've been straight with you, believe me. Trust me on this.'

McIntyre looked deep into his eyes. His instincts had told him he could trust the man. Anyway, what had he to lose but a bit of pride?

Aware of Pike's mocking eyes following him, he strode to the back of the car and lifted the panel that covered the hollow meant to house a spare tyre. Instead of a tyre, six bags of white powder lay snug against each other. McIntyre controlled his excitement, warning himself he'd been duped once already and this could be another piece of duplicity designed to make a fool of him. Only when he slit one of the bags open, dipped a finger in and tasted the powder did he permit himself a satisfied smile. Surely Pike couldn't talk himself out of this.

Displaying a bag in each hand, he moved forward towards Pike. When the gangster saw what he was holding, his smirk vanished.

'There's six bags in total,' McIntyre stated. 'I guess my rabbit pulled out of the hat tops your Rupert the Bear. In fact, you've made a right Rupert of yourself, haven't you, pal?'

McIntyre thought from the gangster's perplexed expression he'd had no idea that there were any drugs in the car, wondered how that could be possible. Then he saw a glimmer of understanding come into his eyes and he stared malevolently at Clancy, who stared back at him impassively.

'You! You did this, Clancy!' he yelled, a shower of spittle coming from his lips. 'I knew all along you were a dirty snout. That's why I

248

set all this up — to see if you'd tell the bizzies.'

Clancy shrugged. 'Don't know what you're talking about. But I know how you feel.' He scratched the back of his head. 'Some guy set me up once. Meant to ask you if you had any idea who that could have been?'

Pike got the message. He looked as though he could kill Clancy on the spot. McIntyre acted quickly, slipping a pair of handcuffs on his wrists and giving him the official spiel. Then he was bundled into the Renault's back seat between McIntyre's colleagues.

'Get on your radio and tell them we want two squad cars here as escorts,' he told the female officer. 'Then we can all go back to headquarters for tea and cream cakes.' Ruefully, he added, 'Hope I have time to digest them before someone arrives and spoils my day.'

31

It was some hours after Pike's arrest that Clancy returned home. It had been an eventful day and he was glad to be back in his house; police stations had too many bad memories for him. When he'd informed McIntyre about the drug deal, the detective had jumped at the chance to set a trap. Fortunately he'd had the foresight to factor in Pike's deviousness. That was why he'd taken out extra insurance and put the drugs in the boot.

Of course, though he had an idea McIntyre suspected what had really happened, his colleagues believed the drugs had been transferred from the Lexus and he didn't intend to dissuade them. Once they found Pike's fingerprints on those bags, given the video evidence they'd gathered, that would be it, all done and dusted. The only anomaly was that when the Lexus had been stopped on the road back to Newcastle they'd found no money. The driver, a small-time burglar, maintained all he'd done was deliver a bag. For Clancy, that confirmed Pike really had been testing him with a dummy run. Finding no money weakened the case, though there was still enough strong evidence for charges of possession with intent to supply to be brought against Pike.

Clancy called out to Joan, who he'd left hidden in the loft. She came down the ladder with obvious relief, anxious to know if his plan had worked out.

'Don't worry, we got him!' he told her. 'Pike will be going to prison.'

The worry lines disappeared and her face lit up. 'I can hardly believe it. After all this time.'

He took her by the hand, led her into the living room, sat her down, explained how Pike would have got away with it if he hadn't been able to use the drugs she'd taken from the gangster's bolt-hole.

'You should have seen his face,' he told her. 'He could see his whole world going up in flames.'

'But it's not over yet, is it?' she said. 'I'll have to testify, stand up in court and let them know about those people he ratted on, identify those policemen he had in his pocket.'

'It'll sink him if you do, lengthen his sentence . . . be a long time before he walks the streets, Joan. You still up for it?'

She managed half a smile. Clancy couldn't

blame her for having reservations. How could it be otherwise when she knew all about Pike's cruel, vengeful nature?

'Testify and everybody will see his true colours. Nobody will want to harm you. They'll be concentrating all their hatred on him. People will want him dead, Joan. You and me, we'll be forgotten.'

She seemed to draw strength from his words and relax a little.

'DI McIntyre is going to set you up in a rehabilitation centre well away from Teesside just as you requested,' Clancy continued. 'He also thinks it best for me to go to a safe house nearby.'

She visibly brightened. 'It's what I wanted, Sam — a chance to be myself again, get clean for good. But what about you? You wanted to stay in Middlesbrough, didn't you?'

Clancy sighed, thinking of the ghosts he was going to leave behind but deep down he knew it was a good thing because living so close to his memories every day wasn't healthy.

'I've thought carefully,' he told her, 'and it's time for me to leave for a while anyway. That apart, I got you into this and it might help you if I'm nearby.'

Joan glanced at him quizzically. 'You know, you've turned out the way I thought you would,' she said. 'I always knew you were a good man. Prison didn't change that.'

Clancy blushed. 'If it hadn't been for my wife's influence, it might have been different. I've been in hell but I know now I can't go back to the old life as I'd imagined I could, not when I remember my wife.'

Joan grimaced. 'God forgive me but that priest deserved to die.'

Fighting back a tear, Clancy said, 'It must have driven Mary out of her mind thinking how she'd left our poor Tom alone with that . . . man.'

Joan kept quiet; simply placed her hand on his arm in a sympathetic gesture.

After a long silence, he said, 'I've come to believe that Mary wouldn't want me to reject my faith. It keeps me straight and gives me hope that I'll see her and little Tommy again. That's all I have left, Joan, all I can do to respect her memory. I'm glad I realized it.'

32

In the bleak surroundings of the interview room, McIntyre faced Pike and his solicitor, Stan Jakeman, across the table. The solicitor was a corpulent figure with the facial expression of an anxious parent on edge because his child is difficult to control and he can't be sure what he'll say or do next. DS Macdonald was sitting next to McIntyre and the tape recorder was already running. Ten minutes in, Pike hadn't admitted anything and the atmosphere was as tense as the final stages of a poker game with a fortune at stake.

'So you still claim you were set up,' McIntyre said wearily. 'Still singing the same old song.'

Pike shrugged. 'You and me both know it.'

With a prolonged sigh, McIntyre leaned back. 'I don't know what you mean. You keep on that theme but when I ask you to elaborate you don't give me anything at all. Doesn't help your case, does it?'

Pike shook his head in exasperation. 'You lot of corrupt bastards fitted me up,' he said, waving a hand in the air. 'Clancy and the bitch were in on it. How else did you know to stop me that day? Clancy planted those drugs but the bitch played a part. Those two were always close.'

'It's much more straightforward,' McIntyre told him. 'Mr Clancy had a change of heart, see, informed us at the last minute.' The detective rubbed his forehead. 'Now you come up with this cock and bull story about testing his loyalty. I ask you . . . going to all that trouble. It beggars belief.'

Pike exchanged glances with his solicitor, who shook his head, warning him he'd said enough on that matter, should let it rest now.

Pike ignored his advice and grunted. 'Clancy put the drugs in the boot.'

'Face the facts, man,' McIntyre came back at him. 'We've found your prints on the bags — your prints, nobody else's. We've got photographs of you getting in the Lexus, then returning to the Mazda carrying a solitary bag and opening the boot.' He smacked his lips together, a connoisseur savouring fine wine. 'Looks bad for you . . . very bad. That amount of drugs, we'll do you for intent to supply.'

'I've told you,' Pike whined. 'I only know there was . . . a toy . . . in the boot.'

'I take it by toy you mean Rupert.'

McIntyre's expression was deadpan but

obviously didn't fool Pike. The twinkle in his eye told him he was winding him up, enjoying doing it.

DS Macdonald started to laugh but converted it to a spluttering cough.

'Sorry,' he said, smiling broadly. 'Tickle in the throat. Probably need some honey.'

McIntyre grinned. 'We contend you hid the drugs in the boot where the spare wheel was kept. As for the presence of the teddy bear ... well, we can only hazard guesses there. Only you really know. People have fetishes. Maybe yours is for teddy bears. On the other hand, as you claim, it could have been a silly practical joke gone wrong.'

'The bear was a joke meant for you lot if you stopped us.'

'That's what you're telling us now,' McIntyre said, winking at him ostentatiously. 'Myself, I believe it was a hangover from your childhood, a comfort need 'cos you think nobody loves you.'

'I must protest,' the solicitor spluttered.

McIntyre realized, out of a desire to see the gangster humiliated, he had gone too far, was verging on the unprofessional, so he held up his hand.

'Interview suspended at 3 p.m.,' he announced and turned the tape off.

Pike and the detective locked eyes across

the table. Jakeman started to say something but a fierce look from Pike silenced him.

'Clancy and the woman,' the gangster muttered. 'They're behind this. They're going to pay them their dues when this is over. You know that, don't you?'

'So threatening behaviour now, is it?' Macdonald chirped up.

McIntyre slid some loose papers into a file, affected an air of nonchalance.

'Don't worry, Mac, the world will soon hear how he set Clancy up, snitched on his rivals. Worse, he was in league with coppers whom he paid to set up anyone who got in his way. His reputation amongst his own kind will fall harder than that statue of Saddam Hussein once that's out.'

Astonishment crept into Pike's face, followed by a shocked expression as though he'd just emerged from a car crash and his life had passed before him, shaking him to the core. His solicitor shuffled in the chair next to him. Rolls of fat wobbled under his shirt as he spoke up.

'Since my client and I are being informed of this for the first time, I take it you will provide the appropriate evidence for ourselves, as is right and proper.'

'Oh, yes,' McIntyre said, the man's verbosity reminding him of John Bright.

'Right and proper it is, Mr Jakeman. Mr Pike deserves no less, being a right and proper person, eh?'

Pike gave his lawyer a scathing glance. McIntyre could see doubt in his eyes. His belief in his own invincibility had been challenged and his ego was struggling with that. Finally, he straightened his shoulders and dragged out each word as though he detested it.

'I've something to say. But I'll only say it off the record and to you alone, McIntyre.'

McIntyre held out his hands, palm upwards. 'Don't think you've anything to say that will make any difference. We've got you dead to rights and you know it.'

Eyes burning, Pike leaned forward. As he did so a drop of sweat dislodged itself from his eyebrow, landed on the curve of his cheek.

'You'll want to hear this,' Pike retorted. 'I'm offering gold.'

The solicitor started to mumble something but Pike made a sharp cutting motion with his hand, aborting whatever he was going to say.

Savouring the gangster's discomfort, McIntyre folded his arms, leaned back lazily, let him sweat some more before he addressed the solicitor and DS Macdonald.

'If he's offering gold, I might as well hear

what he has to say. Can you two leave the room, please?'

The solicitor rose with a warning glance at Pike. Macdonald hesitated and placed a hand on McIntyre's shoulder.

'I'll just be outside, boss, if you need me.'

McIntyre nodded and a moment later he was alone with the man he'd hated for most of his life. It was more than satisfying to see the criminal dressed in standard prison clothes and to think he would soon be paying his dues for all the people he'd exploited. Putting aside those thoughts, he returned to professional mode.

'So it's gold you're offering. Hope it's not fool's gold.'

Pike leaned forward, threading his stubby fingers together.

'I can give you something as good as any gold to you lot but in return I want time taken off if I'm sentenced.'

McIntyre vibrated his bottom lip, shook his head.

'You've been watching too many of those TV cop shows, matey. It doesn't happen that way, not with someone like you.'

'It happens,' Pike said. 'I know it does.'

'Not when we know someone has left a trail of dead men behind him, it doesn't. Poor old Billy Liddle, for one, wouldn't like it. Best

I could offer is better prison conditions, maybe protection inside ... and that's pushing it.'

They stared at each other across the table. Pike started to gnaw at a finger like an animal in pain. Then he glared at the detective and spat on the floor.

'You've had it in for me since me and your brother fell out all those years back. That's the real reason you're not giving me anything here, isn't it?'

'Another copper, same answer,' McIntyre said, with a shrug. 'Nobody can give you what you're asking. I'll do what I can.'

'Your word on that?'

McIntyre nodded. 'Provided what you've got to give is worth anything.'

Pike broke eye contact, stared at the desk top, his brain clearly working out the pros and cons. McIntyre left him alone, didn't attempt to sway him one way or another. Finally, he raised his head, nodded perfunctorily.

'I can give you the names of a lot of bent coppers, photographs, times, places as well.'

McIntyre was impressed. Pike had mentioned gold. This was more like dynamite. The brass would hate the damage done to the force's reputation but to honest policemen dirty coppers were an anathema.

'Write down their names for now,' he told Pike, sliding a pen and paper across the desk.

The gangster picked up the pen, rolled it between his fingers, pondered for a moment then dropped it. For a moment, the detective thought he'd had a change of mind.

'Don't trust you,' Pike grunted. 'I want a letter to say I co-operated, gave you names and places, compromising photographs. When I have that, my solicitor will hand you all I have on your workmates.'

The provision of photographs would add an extra bit of glitter to the gold. Photographs usually meant blackmail. Pike had probably had them taken to make sure the coppers he'd used stayed on board. Their information had likely enabled him to evade the traps set for him.

'Fair enough. I'll have one drawn up but there'll be nothing about better conditions or protection. You'll just have to accept I'll argue your case, much as it'll stick in my craw. Oh, and one more thing. Anyone hurts Sam Clancy or Joan Burton, it won't happen.'

Pike pursed his lips, looking more like a grumpy old man than a tough gangster. He was clearly not enthusiastic about the arrangement. Underneath an impassive exterior, McIntyre was enjoying seeing the gangster cornered like one of those lower-tier criminals he'd thought himself above all these years.

'You'll get the names and photographs from my solicitor soon as I have proof I co-operated with you bastards,' the gangster said eventually.

'Agreed! That's us done then.'

The room fell silent. McIntyre could feel the past pervading the silence, all that had passed between them over the years telescoping into that room, that moment. He felt like a marathon runner after a long, arduous race, the finishing line at last in view. Judging from Pike's morose expression, the reality of his situation was filtering through, the delusion of invulnerability that sustained him in his dog-eat-dog world crumbling.

'Two boys from Grove Hill,' Pike muttered eventually in an effort to rally. 'How come we ended up so different?'

McIntyre looked him in the eye and sighed. 'If we're getting philosophical, I suppose I'd begin with your old man. He didn't exactly give you a good start. Whip a dog to make it fight, it turns out bad.'

Pike nodded, as though he needed to latch on to something, anything, to make sense of his impending fate. Was there a seed of conscience in him, after all? McIntyre wondered, surprised to see a reflective side he could never have imagined Pike possessed.

'Yeah, you were the lucky one,' the gangster opined, his tone envious. 'Your father treated you better than my father treated me.'

'Sure he did,' McIntyre agreed. 'But what if the dog wanted to fight anyway? Nothing would have made a difference.'

In spite of those words, remembering the way Pike's father treated him, the detective couldn't help feeling a sliver of pity for the man who'd been his enemy. Upbringing, the luck of the draw, genetics? Who could say what exactly dictated how a man turned out. But it wasn't something he'd be losing sleep over. Too much thought like that and he wouldn't be able to do his job properly.

'Analyze it all you like,' he continued. 'In the end, you brought misery to too many lives, no doubt ended some, never a thought for your victims or their families, just yourself. Now you'll have a long time to think about that.'

Pike didn't answer. McIntyre figured he had nothing else to say and their business was concluded. Yet when he rose and moved towards the door, Pike called after him.

'What about your Paul?'

The detective turned on his heel, hackles rising. He was sure Pike was going to return to form, attempt to hurt him by referring to his brother in a derogatory way.

'What?'

'Could easily have ended up like me, that lad,' Pike muttered. 'Same family as you, different result.'

McIntyre frowned. He didn't intend to prolong the conversation, insult his beloved brother's memory by discussing him with this criminal.

'Paul was way above your league,' he snapped, edging out of the door. 'No way he'd have sunk to your level.'

33

A week after interviewing Pike, McIntyre drove to work in a better mood than he'd known in an age. Something, maybe the feeling the dice were rolling for him at last, made him change direction and head to Kate's place. He hadn't heard from her and had stayed away deliberately, avoided even telephoning, to give her time to come to terms with her brother's arrest. But he felt he was ready now to make a move, discover where he stood with her after all the craziness.

It was helpful he understood the reason for her previous ambivalence towards him, and he hoped she saw him in a different light. It had certainly seemed that way the night her brother had been arrested, but her heightened emotional state could have been responsible for her change of heart, the reconciliation that had taken place. Anyway, he could but hope and further procrastination wouldn't help him.

Sitting in the Done Roaming car park, his previous resolve soon weakened and he didn't feel so confident. Had he given her enough

265

time? he wondered. Would she still be too preoccupied with her brother's problems? Did her silence since that awful night mean he would receive a negative response from her? In the end, figuring he'd leave it a few more days, he started the engine — but just as he put his foot on the accelerator, Kate suddenly emerged from the main building and headed toward her flat. Her appearance changed his mind once again. Turning the engine off, he got out of the car, strode towards her flat and knocked on the door.

It didn't take long for her to answer and he was relieved when, before he had spoken a word, she greeted him with a smile and an invitation to come inside and have a coffee. Seated in the kitchen, he watched her, thinking she looked much more herself than on the night of her brother's arrest. But when she sat down opposite him he could detect a certain shy reserve which he didn't think augured well.

After a few pleasantries, an awkward silence developed between them and they avoided eye contact. McIntyre's gaze drifted to the window just as grey clouds drifted over the sun, making the kitchen suddenly darker and gloomier. It quickly emerged again in its full glory, which didn't last because, like guardians jealous of its lustre, the clouds soon closed ranks again. McIntyre felt himself vacillate between optimism and pessimism as he tried to read Kate's mood. Finally, he took a deep breath and stepped into delicate territory.

'You must have been to see your brother?'

She closed her eyes fleetingly. 'Yes, I visited him. It wasn't pleasant seeing him shut away.'

'I can imagine.'

'But,' she added, 'deep down I always knew it was going to end like that. I was in denial . . . before.'

The sun made another sally, bathing her face in light. Then a bird swooped past the window. Its wings cast a fluttering shadow across her cheek which seemed to momentarily startle her. She narrowed her eyes, shuddered.

'My brother could have ended up dead in some back alley.'

McIntyre, not sure what to say, kept his answer short.

'It happens, Kate.'

She opened her eyes wide, stared at a point somewhere over his shoulder with an agonized expression. Something told him she was seeing her brother's corpse, a needle sticking out of his arm like a grave marker, a warning to all who passed that way. For a few moments she remained oblivious to his presence. Then she blinked and focused on him again.

'If he'd died I would never have forgiven myself for shielding him, giving him money to feed his habit.' A solitary tear coursed down her cheek. 'If that poor old man he struck hadn't recovered . . . '

McIntyre's intuition told him the reason why she hadn't been in touch with him these last few days was the fact that she was embarrassed, blaming herself, finding it hard to forgive herself.

'He's your brother, Kate. Only natural to help your kin. Tough love doesn't come easy. You have to realize that and . . . try to go easy on yourself.'

She managed a semblance of a smile. 'He's agreed to have counselling and wants to be on the drug-free wing of the prison. It's a positive step, the first I can remember in an age.'

'That is good news, Kate. It'll work for him if he really makes up his mind he wants it to. It sounds that he does.'

She frowned and looked worried again.

'I hope he's not stringing everybody along, pretending he wants to change.'

It was a possibility, McIntyre knew. He'd seen it happen, prisoners making all the right noises, going on the right courses, drug awareness, anger control, the whole plethora, and not for genuine motives but in the hope of gaining an early release. But he wasn't going to say anything to worry Kate so he changed the subject, told her how Pike, the man who had manipulated her brother, would be put away for a long time. He decided it wasn't the time to bring up their own future and he should go, but she spoke before he had a chance to take his leave.

'I couldn't bring myself to contact you, Don,' she said, dropping her eyes. 'I know I should have done.'

It felt a bit like the opener for a Dear John letter, a gentle shove rather than a big push but the same result in the end. He squared his shoulders ready to face up to it, walk away with no hard feelings.

'I apologize for that,' she continued. 'The reason is I'm embarrassed about the dreadful way I behaved towards you, how I'd misjudged you. After all my nonsense, you took a big chance for me when I didn't deserve it.'

'No need,' he said. 'It's all forgotten. Remember I had a brother who could do no wrong in my eyes so I do understand because I would probably have done the same for Paul as you did for your brother.'

She looked him straight in the eye. 'I

wouldn't have blamed you if you'd walked away.'

That remark gave him a natural way to broach what he really wanted to discuss with her.

'Has all that's happened made any difference to you and me, Kate? Can we make a fresh start, do you think?'

'We understand each other better,' she said, smiling. 'If you can put what has happened behind you, then I can.'

'It's already miles behind me,' he said, making a show of looking over his shoulder. 'The dust clouds are disappearing already.'

After that, with the air cleared, they were both much more relaxed and agreed they'd have a night out soon. McIntyre hadn't realized how much time had passed and, glancing at his watch, realized he'd better head into the office or they'd be wondering where he was. One good thing was his stock was pretty high at work. Snaith was the exception there, of course. He'd phoned to congratulate him on solving the priest's murder but in a tone so perfunctory he might as well not have bothered. Fortunately, when Pike was arrested, the DCI was away at a conference but he was due back at any time and McIntyre figured there'd be a price to pay for using his initiative. His excuse would be there was no time to pass his information through normal channels and the chance to catch Pike had been too good an opportunity to miss.

Kate walked him to the door. Just as he was about to depart, she put her hand to her mouth, told him she'd remembered something. Leaving him on the step, she went back inside and emerged holding a brown envelope.

'What's this?' he said, grinning. 'Not my P45, is it? Not after we just made our peace pact.'

'Norman gave it to me,' she said, referring to the old boy her brother had struck. 'He was friendly with your aunt, remember. She asked him to give this to you if anything happened to her. His memory isn't too good and he forgot; only remembered when he saw you that night.'

He slid the envelope inside his coat pocket. 'Probably be one of her famous recipes,' he said, kissing Kate on the cheek.

He waved at her as he drove away and, as he passed the sign at the exit, he wondered if, at last, Done Roaming might apply to him.

34

Back at work, after a tedious spell of paperwork, for a change of routine he listened to the messages on his answer-phone. There was one from an irate Jimmy Snaith. He said he'd be coming to see McIntyre tomorrow in his office at 10 a.m. sharp, the subject of his visit his outrageous behaviour pertaining to the arrest of Tony Pike. McIntyre wasn't surprised; he had been expecting it.

Mid-morning he popped out for a breather and when he returned he found Pike's fat solicitor, Stan Jakeman, waiting for him outside his office, briefcase clutched under his arm. No love lost between them because they'd clashed on too many occasions, they shook hands merely as a matter of form. McIntyre was glad to see him, however, figuring he'd come to deliver the letter Pike had promised. Best all that was out of the way before Snaith descended on him breathing fire. The letter Pike had requested in return was drawn up and in his desk drawer.

'I assume you have something from Pike?' he asked Jakeman as they entered the office. 'Or you wouldn't be here.'

'Your assumption is correct,' Jakeman agreed. 'Mr Pike has drawn up his list and there are appropriate photographs with it.'

They sat down facing each other and the solicitor extracted an envelope from his briefcase, which he placed on the desk.

'It's all there for you, DI McIntyre, all the dirty washing laid out to dry.'

It was said with a sly satisfaction because their business pertained to corrupt policemen and Jakeman was drawing perverse enjoyment from the fact. Restraining himself from making a comment, he unlocked his drawer and pulled out a smaller envelope.

'I'll give you this once I've seen what he's offering,' he said, waving it at the solicitor.

Jakeman gave a supercilious smile. 'I'm sure that you'll find it all to your satisfaction . . . or perhaps I should say to your dissatisfaction.'

McIntyre sighed. 'Unlike some who make a career, not to mention money, out of the law, I'm only interested in seeing those who break it punished . . . whoever they are.' He reached for the envelope, stared meaningfully at the solicitor, then shook his head. 'Don't know how you can stand representing a man like Pike. The smell must linger.'

Jakeman shrugged his indifference. 'Everyone deserves a defence. You really should clean up the water you're swimming in, Detective, before you criticize others. I think you'll find the smell of your own stinking fish hard to stomach.' He grinned like a shark. 'Please open the envelope so we can proceed.'

McIntyre didn't bother replying. Anxious to peruse the envelope's contents, he slit it open and pulled out a list of names with a clutch of photographs. He ran his finger down the list and when he came to the fifth he couldn't hide his shocked reaction. Glancing at the fat man, he saw his shoulders shaking with amusement.

'That's rocked your world, eh, Detective?' he chortled.

Ignoring him, McIntyre returned his attention to the list. Written underneath were times and dates Pike had met those he'd corrupted and a summary of the information he'd paid for on each occasion. That fifth name featured more than the others. It all felt unreal as he flicked through the photographs, which were clear visual evidence of the meetings, the features of those involved easily recognizable.

When he raised his head, Jakeman pulled out his wallet and with a smirk flicked his business card across the table.

'I'm not proud, Detective. Any of your

colleagues need representing, tell them I'm available.'

McIntyre was floored, didn't know what to say, so made do with a disdainful glower as he slid his own envelope across the table. Jakeman opened it and scrutinized the contents.

'Scant reward, really,' he said, sliding it into his briefcase and heaving himself out of the chair.

'Tell that to your golden goose.'

Jakeman waddled to the door and paused there. 'Sadly the golden goose is dead to me now.' He shook his head. 'But you never know, perhaps I'll find one who lays bigger eggs.'

'Shameless,' McIntyre said, as he closed the door. 'Utterly shameless.'

McIntyre, feeling as though he was in a dream and would soon wake up, sat back and thought about what he'd just learned. Life certainly had its surprises.

35

Next morning McIntyre deliberately arrived at work at 9.45 a.m. Snaith's car wasn't in the car park so he parked in the street and waited. The DCI turned up five minutes before 10 a.m. but McIntyre didn't drive in until a few minutes past the hour. When he glanced up at his office window, he saw Snaith watching him from that vantage point but still took his time parking up. Then he ambled towards the building as though he had all the time in the world, his intention to rile the DCI with a show of indifference to his presence.

Standing outside the Incident Room a few minutes later, he peeked through the glass door. Mac, Moira, Bird and several others were beavering away at their desks. He could sense a calmer atmosphere in the room than recently, knew it was because they were focused on clearing up the mountain of paperwork that had piled up during the recent investigations; there was none of the frenetic bustling that attended a work in progress evident now. There wasn't much chance he could cross the room unseen but he tried, slipping through the door and manoeuvring his way through spaces separating the desks while staring straight ahead. But he soon heard the whispers start up and his peripheral vision was aware of heads swivelling. Giving up his futile attempt at invisibility, he looked round the room. His colleagues started to point to his office at the far end, screwing up their noses as though there was a rotten smell coming from that direction. He knew the reason for their behaviour and though they'd hardly have been flattered at the idea, they reminded him of a gang of monkeys drawing attention to the fact there was a rogue male on their territory and indicating their displeasure at the intrusion. In a way, he was flattered by their spontaneous display of loyalty but his only response was to wave a hand vaguely and keep going, hoping he wouldn't need to stop. Moira, however, had other ideas and stepped in front of him.

'What are you playing at, boss?' she exclaimed, a concerned look on her face. 'The DCI is in your office and he's fuming. He says you had an appointment at 10 a.m. He's been sounding off asking us where you were and none of us had a clue. He was like a madman. You'd better get your excuses ready.'

McIntyre grinned.

'I'm due a really severe reprimand this time, Moira, so don't you think it should be his office, no coffee?'

Moira gave an exasperated sigh, shook her head. 'Either way, you're doing yourself no favours. He's a dangerous enemy, that man. He'll have your guts for garters, mood he's in. You need to be prepared to defend yourself, not grinning like an idiot.'

'Don't worry about me, lass,' he said, touched by her concern. 'Watch this space. He'll be the one who comes out of that room with his guts spilling out of his stomach, believe me.'

Without further explanation he stepped around her, continued on his way, aware of the hushed whispers behind him. For sure, those present would be anticipating fireworks now, especially if they'd heard that last remark.

He found Snaith in his chair . . . again. He was in full uniform, cap on his head, hands on the desk, thumbs circling each other. When he saw the DI, his cheeks turned a deeper shade of red and his eyes fired missiles in McIntyre's direction, preliminary signals for an impending verbal attack. But he was forestalled by his DI making the first incursion.

'Keeping my chair warm, are we, sir?' McIntyre's sarcastic tone was unmistakable as he sat down opposite his superior. 'Don't need a bum warmer when you're around, do I?'

Snaith's thumbs ceased their manic rotating. Flummoxed by the junior officer's insolence, he was stumped for a reply. Then, when he managed to find his voice, his words came out in a stutter.

'I'm . . . s-sick of you and your attitude, McIntyre. Who do you think . . . you are?'

McIntyre angled his head to the side. 'I think I'm just one of many conscientious cops in the force, sir. I'm sure you've met them in your time.'

Snaith's brow furrowed. He clenched his fists and thrust his jaw forward.

'First off,' he said, voice raised, 'I told you I was coming to your office, gave you a time and you've turned up twenty minutes late.'

McIntyre feigned puzzlement. 'I wouldn't have minded coming to your office, sir, really I wouldn't. That's what usually happens when someone's in big trouble. Were you just being kind coming to me like this?'

Snaith looked more bemused than ever and obviously couldn't believe McIntyre had the temerity to bait him. He took off his cap and slammed it down on the table. Unimpressed by the histrionics, McIntyre just grinned, figuring the man was trying to gain time to work out a suitable response.

'Well, that's the last straw,' he said eventually, 'the one that's going to break the camel's back, in case there's any doubt!'

McIntyre eyed him. 'You really have got the hump with me, haven't you, sir?'

Snaith was already bemused, now he looked dazed. If he'd been in a boxing ring he'd have been sent to a corner because his jaw went slack, his mouth dropped open and his eyelids fluttered like a bird's wings. McIntyre had skirted the borders of outright insubordination in the past, but this was taking it to a new level and his voice shook as he spoke.

'You did a good job finding the priest killer. Congratulations were in order, plaudits from on high. I was spreading the word.' He reached for his cap, ran a finger along the peak as though testing a blade. 'I should have known better, should have known that undisciplined maverick streak of yours would kick in and ruin things.' He dropped his cap on the desk, cuffed it away from him in a show of temper. 'You were told in no uncertain terms to lay off Pike, yet you went ahead without permission, arranged his arrest on your tod, in flagrant disobedience of my orders.'

McIntyre conjured up a pained expression. 'No plaudits from on high for me, then, even though we got a man we'd been after for years?'

Snaith breathed heavily. Like a bull prior to a charge, his nostrils dilated and contracted.

'I'm here to inform you that I intend the severest disciplinary procedures against you,' he said, drawing back his shoulders.

'Don't like the sound of that,' McIntyre replied. 'But I'll take consolation from the fact I won't be alone in my misery, sir, because you'll be right there at my side.'

The DCI's eyes showed a glimmer of fear. His voice was hoarse, an undercurrent of fear there too. 'What rubbish are you talking now?'

McIntyre reached inside his jacket, extracted an envelope, threw it down on the desk like a gauntlet.

'What's this, another of your puerile games?'

Snaith reached for the envelope, tried for a condescending smile, which came as a mere twitch of his lips.

'Suck it and see,' McIntyre told him.

The DCI opened the envelope, tipped out the contents, stared at the photographs lying on the desk as though he'd been served a foreign dish and, though tempted, was reluctant to take even a bite in case it offended his palate. Then, reluctantly, he succumbed, reached out and spread the photographs, inspected each in turn, growing increasingly pale with each viewing. When he finished, he stared vacantly into space. He seemed to have aged ten years.

'Didn't know you were so photogenic,' McIntyre said, showing him no mercy. 'Pike, on the other hand, let's just say he's not a pretty picture in any context. You sort of put him in the shade though.'

'Where did you get these?' Snaith asked, a quake in his voice.

'From your lord and master, of course. You should have expected as much when you decided to consort with him. He thinks exposing you will give him advantages.'

As though he was trying to follow a bird's erratic flight, Snaith's eyes darted desperately in all directions except McIntyre's. The DI watched him, thinking that if he was trying to find a way to explain himself he had no chance. It took him a long time to speak and when he did his eyes bored into McIntyre's as though he was still top dog and could dominate the DI by sheer force of will.

'It's true. I did meet Pike a few times, off

my own bat, to try to convince him to turn against his rivals. It isn't recorded unfortunately.' He pointed to the photographs. 'All this really shows is that I've been a maverick — at times — like yourself.'

McIntyre just smiled. Even though there was satisfaction exposing this man's duplicity, he felt a certain sadness too, listening to one of their own trying to wriggle like one of the criminals he dealt with every day.

'None of that rubbish will help you,' he said. 'Two of those photographs show you receiving a package from Pike — money, perchance? He's written everything down, times, dates, etc., and he'll sing loud and clear to help himself. Your financial affairs will be scrutinized. Wonder what they'll turn up there?'

McIntyre had him. The DCI knew it. His shoulders slumped forward and he stared glassily at the DI as though in his mind he was seeing a cold, lonely landscape that he'd have to cross into a shameful exile.

'It's been a long time coming,' McIntyre said. 'In the old days, I wondered whether you were bent. Now I understand why Pike slipped away from me so many times at the last moment, why you were so keen to take me off his case. He trained you like a pet monkey, didn't he?'

Snaith didn't protest. He was bereft of words. McIntyre placed the photographs back in the envelope, stood up and looked down on the DCI, his face impassive.

'DCI Snaith, I am arresting you on charges of corruption. You do not have to say anything now but . . . '

Snaith didn't move a muscle. McIntyre gave him the spiel verbatim, gripped his elbow, told him to stand up. He made no fuss, rose mechanically, that absent look still in his eyes, evidently already cutting himself off from the world he'd known.

McIntyre had arranged for two uniforms to be waiting for them. As he led Snaith into the Incident Room, they were hovering outside the glass door on the far side. He beckoned to them and, while his colleagues watched in stunned silence, walked Snaith to the middle of the room where the uniforms met him.

'Take the prisoner down to the custody sergeant,' he announced. 'He's been briefed to expect a new arrival.'

The two uniforms positioned themselves either side of Snaith. He kept his head bowed as they led him to the door. When they'd disappeared from sight the room remained in silence, the kind that occurs at the denouement of a play which has left the audience hanging in the air, not knowing what to think.

McIntyre stood alone in the spotlight, conscious of uncomprehending stares in his direction. He wanted to explain but the words wouldn't come because, at the end of the day, Snaith was one of their own who had deceived them. Figuring they'd find out soon enough, he headed for the door. What he needed most was fresh air.

36

That night, a whisky in his hand, McIntyre sat in the dark staring out of the window of his flat, thinking over the day's events. With Pike in prison, Snaith likely to join him, two adversaries were vanishing from his life and he felt a chapter was closing. His gaze drifted to the silhouette of the Cleveland Hills on the horizon. The shape they formed reminded him of a man lying on his back, resting after a hard day's work. He could identify with that image right now but it also reminded him how so much in his professional and personal life had been pure illusion. Scratch the surface, nothing had been the way it seemed initially.

John Bright, for instance, had been living a lie, conning staff and students. The priest and his bishop, who would soon be facing charges himself, were hypocrites betraying their faith. Snaith was as corrupt as they come. Even Kate had assumed a false persona with him, though for a good reason. His mind turned to Sam Clancy, for whom he felt a great deal of sympathy. That man had been dealt a rotten hand, been imprisoned on a false presumption, and the priest he had trusted cost him the lives of his wife and son.

Policemen were often accused of being cynics, he reflected, and perhaps it was no wonder when human beings were hardly ever what they seemed to be. That thought brought his father to mind, because he considered him as near to an exception as you could find. A good, dependable man, his only flaw had been that when trouble had come to his door he'd run from it and the cycle that had destroyed their family had begun.

After his second whisky, he decided enough was enough and retired to the bedroom, closed the curtains and started to undress. That was when he noticed the envelope. It was poking out of the inside pocket of the jacket he'd left hanging behind the door. Slightly fuzzy-headed from the whisky, he couldn't remember putting it there until it clicked that Kate had given it to him. Pressure of work must have made him forget about it. He decided it could wait until morning but then his conscience started to niggle. His aunt had been dear to him and it seemed disrespectful to delay opening it any longer. She'd been a sentimental old girl, so probably it would be an old photograph she wanted him to have.

He climbed into bed with the envelope in his hand, propped himself up on the pillow, opened it and found that it contained another envelope that had already been opened. It had a Ministry of Defence logo and was addressed to his father at his old Wolviston home. Judging from its crumpled condition, it had been read more than once. With his curiosity aroused, he started to read the typed letter it contained.

The words went through his brain like a sweeping scythe, cutting away at his past beliefs until he felt sick, but not from the whisky he'd drunk. The portent of what was written destroyed a myth he'd manufactured in his mind and a vortex of emotions swirled in his head as he realized how deluded he'd been.

Over and over again he read the letter until the words started to blur. Then he lay in the dark plagued by his guilt because while he had been unravelling the deceits of other people, he'd been deceiving himself for years. An old detective once told him never to be in a hurry to judge. That he had done so hurt now like a physical wound. Sleep wouldn't come. Snippets of memories he'd dismissed long ago came back to him like fragments of a photograph torn up too hastily. One memory loomed larger than the others; Paul being brought home drunk by a policeman. He'd watched events from the top stair, seen his father gripping the departing bobby's hand and heard him thanking him profusely. During the following days Paul hadn't been himself, he remembered, was unusually quiet. Not long afterwards, the fight in the park had occurred. That move to Wolviston, for which he'd blamed his father, had soon followed. Now he understood everything and felt ashamed of himself.

37

Mid-morning the next day, tired from a restless night and the weight of a conscience he was finding heavy to bear, McIntyre arrived at his father's flat. A plump man with his shirt sleeves rolled up to the elbow opened the door when he knocked. At first, he didn't recognize the florid face but the stethoscope hanging around his neck was a giveaway; the man was a doctor he'd come in contact with during the course of his work. Already filled with trepidation, in the moment of silence that followed, he feared his father had been taken ill, might even have died. The spasm that gripped his stomach only relented when the doctor smiled because surely he wouldn't be smiling if the worst had happened. But what was the doctor doing here?

Before the doctor had a chance to explain, he asked, 'What's wrong? Is my father ill?'

The doctor shook his head reassuringly. 'No need for you to worry. He had a little turn in the street the other day and the nurse asked me to pop in to examine him. He's all right and he's just getting dressed now.'

'Little turn?' McIntyre repeated anxiously, as he followed the doctor inside.

'A mild angina attack . . . he gets them from time to time . . . but we're managing them with medication.' The doctor looked at him curiously. 'Didn't you know?'

He followed the doctor into the living room where his father was standing by the fireplace buttoning his shirt. McIntyre thought he looked older, more tired than when he'd seen him last. Or was he imagining that because he'd just been told his father, whom he'd always considered pretty indestructible, was having trouble with his heart?

'Why didn't you tell me?' McIntyre reproached him, then added more softly, 'You should have told me.'

His father straightened. 'You're a busy man, son, didn't want to bother you. Anyway it's nowt but my old ticker reminding me I'm mortal . . . as if I didn't know.'

The doctor picked his bag off the sofa. 'You'll be fine if you take your pills and don't push yourself too hard,' he commented, glancing at McIntyre as he moved towards the door. 'Don't worry, I'll find my own way out. You stay with your father. Sounds to me as though you need to have a talk with him.'

When they were alone, his father sat down

in his armchair. 'A lot of fuss over nothing much,' he mumbled. 'I'm not even worth one of those tents, they reckon.'

'Stents not tents,' McIntyre corrected him irritably.

His father was making it clear in his own way that he didn't want to discuss the matter further but McIntyre didn't like the fact he'd kept his condition from him. As had become only too clear, the old boy was well practised at holding back to his own detriment.

'You tell me about things like this in future,' he said, adding more meaningfully, 'and anything else I should know.'

His father gave a perfunctory nod. 'Anyway, what are you doing here?'

McIntyre hesitated. He wasn't sure how his father would take it when he revealed he'd read the letter and he found himself delaying the moment.

'Thought you'd like to know I got Pike in the cells facing a long prison term. All the gremlins are coming out of the walls and turning against him. He's scared, pathetic and coughing up names you wouldn't believe.'

His father considered the news, then said, 'Well, then, I'm pleased for you. He was the reason I made us move, it's true. Though you haven't mentioned it for a long while now, I know you've always held that against me and hated Pike. Maybe now you can forget your obsession with him. It wasn't ever . . . healthy.'

'If I'd known the truth, perhaps he wouldn't have got under my skin to that extent,' McIntyre said, seizing the opening. 'But I was on the wrong track because you never told me the whole truth, did you?'

His father's eyes widened. He shifted uncomfortably in his chair. McIntyre knew why he was so disconcerted; he was afraid the secret he'd been hiding from his son had come to light after a long hibernation.

'Don't know what you mean, son.'

McIntyre shook his head. It was just like his old man to be stubborn to the last.

'You know what I mean, all right. You see, I know about Paul and the real reason we moved to Wolviston.'

His father looked surprised but he was still willing to prevaricate.

'I did what I thought best at the time. Pike wasn't the type to let Paul rest after their fight, would have got to him eventually. That type always do. He might even have tried to get back at him through you. I wasn't having any of that . . . so we moved. You know this, so why stir up all that again?'

It was half the truth. McIntyre knew he was

holding back so much more.

'I thought you were a bit of a coward for running away,' he told his father, 'and you let me believe it.'

'So you told me more than a few times,' his father snapped. 'I didn't want to leave Grove Hill any more than you did, but I don't regret it for one moment.'

McIntyre sighed. 'But you still haven't told me everything. Even now you're just feeding me scraps!'

He reached inside his jacket, withdrew the letter and waved it at his father. The old man instantly gathered what it contained because he covered his face with his hands. McIntyre gave him time and a silence developed until eventually he lowered his hands, gave a resigned sigh and, with obvious reluctance, met his son's eye.

'I presume you gave this to my aunt so I'd never see it, probably made her promise not to show it to me. Wisely, she made sure I received it after her death. Otherwise I'd never have known the truth, would I?'

His father stared at the carpet and McIntyre was conscious of old ghosts in the room with them, ghosts who could never be far from them, but closing in now to hear old hurts finally put to bed so the living and the dead could rest easier.

'As you'll recall, this letter is from the MOD, addressed to you.' His voice was gentle, carrying no hint of reproach. 'Paul left it for his next of kin, to be delivered only if he was killed in action. After all that's passed I think we should hear it together.

'*Dear Father,*' he began, before the old man could object. '*First, I need to thank you for everything you've done for me, you and Mother both. I was so proud of being your son, I think that when you told me I was adopted it sent me off the rails for a while. Moving me away from the town, then encouraging me to join the army, was the best thing. It set me on a better path. The life has suited me and, if it all ends badly, remember I was doing what I wanted to do. I have no regrets, neither should you.*'

McIntyre swallowed hard. The next paragraph referred to him and every time he'd read it he'd felt a lump rising in his throat. Fighting tears, he pressed on.

'*Don will take my death hard. I know he thought too much of me but his love was reciprocated. You left it to me to tell my brother I was adopted, in my own time, you suggested, but I could never do it. I would consider it an honour if you could find it in your heart to let him always go on thinking I am his blood brother and remember me as* such because I feel as close to him as I could to anyone in this world. I would be grateful, too, if he remained ignorant of the way I let you down, so that he only remembers the best part of me.

'Words cannot express my love for my family, my gratitude for sacrifices you made. Don't grieve for me. Think of me as someone you set on the right path, who is now with your wife, my mother, in a place where I hope we'll meet again.'

McIntyre placed the letter on his lap, swallowed hard. 'Your loving son, Paul.'

His father raised his head for the first time since McIntyre had begun reading.

'He was adopted,' he muttered, superfluously. 'He didn't want you to know that but now you do.'

'Doesn't matter. Never would have. He should have known.'

The door to the past had been thrown wide open. Now McIntyre wanted to see everything that lay behind it and this was the time.

'That night the policeman brought Paul home drunk. Something happened. I don't know what, but it had repercussions, changed things for us. I'd like you to tell me about it.'

His father glared at him but, as though reconciled to the fact that there was no need to hide secrets any more, his expression soon

ned. Clearing his throat, he began his

er I told Paul he was adopted, he got in
ike, started hiding things for him. One
that policeman found Paul drunk with
stolen goods on him. Fortunately he
an old pal of mine, knew Paul had no
ous, said he'd give him another chance,
rt that he'd found the stuff in a hedge.'
Don't tell me,' McIntyre interrupted. 'The
t was over the stolen goods. Pike wanted
m and Paul couldn't provide them. Pike
uldn't afford to lose face.'
His father nodded. 'A few days later Paul
onfessed he'd been taking drugs. I was
worried about him, also that he might
influence you the wrong way, decided enough
was enough.' His father sighed. 'You know the
rest.'

Learning how his father had tried to protect Paul and his real motivation in moving
his family, McIntyre felt ashamed of the way
he'd misjudged him. Why hadn't he come
clean instead of allowing him to interpret it as
cowardly without ever correcting him? Not
only that, but persuading Paul to join the
army, tragic as it had proved in the long run,
had been sensible too, given the situation.

'Couldn't you have told me . . . something?' he said, his voice desiccated.

'You read the letter. Paul's last wishes
cerning you were clear enough. I wasn't
to lie and I wasn't going to deny him w
wanted.' His father looked sad. 'He w
son from cradle to grave, no matter wha

Those words touched McIntyre's
Overcome with emotion, he couldn't
back any longer and placed a hand o
father's shoulder.

'I'm so sorry,' he said. 'All these years
allowed myself to think wrong things. I sho
have known. Can you ever forgive me?'

His father gave him a sharp look. 'You
my son, aren't you? I know you're a good la
just like Paul. There's nothing to forgive. I
just the way it was.'

They sat in companionable silence for a
while, McIntyre figuring there was a lot he
had to be forgiven for but much more at ease
than he'd felt for a long time.

'There's so much that people have going
on we don't see,' he said eventually.

'You're referring to Paul and me, are you,
son?'

'Yes, but everybody, Dad, everybody. We
only see the tip of the iceberg. I intend to
keep that much more in mind from now on
before I rush to judge them.'

His father smiled. 'You're halfway to
finding wisdom, son.'